THE WORLD'S CLASSICS

A GENTLE CREATURE
AND OTHER STORIES

FYODOR MIKHAILOVICH DOSTOEVSKY was born in Moscow in 1821, the second in a family of seven children. His mother died of consumption in 1837 and his father, a generally disliked army physician, was murdered on his estate two years later. In 1844 he left the College of Military Engineering in St Petersburg and devoted himself to writing. *Poor Folk* (1846) met with great success from the literary critics of the day. In 1849 he was imprisoned and sentenced to death on account of his involvement with a group of utopian socialists, the Petrashevsky Circle. The sentence was commuted at the last moment to penal servitude and exile, but the experience radically altered his political and personal ideology and led directly to *Memoirs from the House of the Dead* (1861–2). In 1857, while still in exile, he married his first wife, Maria Dmitrievna Isaeva, returning to St Petersburg in 1859. In the early 1860s he founded two new literary journals, *Vremia* and *Epokha*, and proved himself to be a brilliant journalist. He travelled in Europe, which served to strengthen his anti-European sentiment. During this period abroad he had an affair with Polina Suslova, the model for many of his literary heroines, including Polina in *The Gambler*. Central to their relationship was their mutual passion for gambling—an obsession which brought financial chaos to his affairs. Both his wife and his much-loved brother, Mikhail, died in 1864, the same year in which *Notes from the Underground* was published; *Crime and Punishment* and *The Gambler* followed in 1866 and in 1867 he married his stenographer, Anna Snitkina, who managed to bring an element of stability into his frenetic life. His other major novels, *The Idiot* (1868), *Devils* (1871), and *The Karamazov Brothers* (1880) met with varying degrees of success. In 1880 he was hailed as a saint, prophet, and genius by the audience to whom he delivered an address at the unveiling of the Pushkin memorial. He died seven months later in 1881; at the funeral thirty thousand people accompanied his coffin and his death was mourned throughout Russia.

ALAN MYERS has translated a wide variety of contemporary Russian texts. His versions of Joseph Brodsky include poetry and prose collected in *A Part of Speech* and *Less than One*, as well as his plays *Marbles* and *Democracy*. He has also published *An Age Ago*, an anthology from the golden age of Russian poetry. His translation of *The Idiot* by Fyodor Dostoevsky is also in World's Classics.

WILLIAM LEATHERBARROW is Professor of Russian at the University of Sheffield. His publications include *Fedor Dostoevsky: A Reference Guide* (Boston, Mass., 1990), *Dostoyevsky: The Brothers Karamazov* (Cambridge, 1992) and *Dostoevskii and Britain* (forthcoming).

DOSTOEVSKY IN WORLD'S CLASSICS

An Accidental Family (A Raw Youth)

Crime and Punishment

Devils

The Idiot

The Karamazov Brothers

Memoirs from the House of the Dead

Notes from the Underground

A Gentle Creature and Other Stories

THE WORLD'S CLASSICS

FYODOR DOSTOEVSKY

White Nights
A Gentle Creature
The Dream of a Ridiculous Man

Translated by
ALAN MYERS

With an Introduction by
W. J. LEATHERBARROW

Oxford New York
OXFORD UNIVERSITY PRESS
1995

Oxford University Press, Walton Street, Oxford OX2 6DP

Oxford New York
Athens Auckland Bangkok Bombay
Calcutta Cape Town Dar es Salaam Delhi
Florence Hong Kong Istanbul Karachi
Kuala Lumpur Madras Madrid Melbourne
Mexico City Nairobi Paris Singapore
Taipei Tokyo Toronto
and associated companies in
Berlin Ibadan

Oxford is a trade mark of Oxford University Press

Translation, Note on the Translation, Explanatory Notes © Alan Myers 1995
Introduction © W. J. Leatherbarrow 1995

First published as a World's Classics Paperback 1995

British Library Cataloguing in Publication Data
Data available

Library of Congress Cataloging in Publication Data
Data available
ISBN 0-19-282280-2

1 3 5 7 9 10 8 6 4 2

Typeset by CentraCet Limited, Cambridge
Printed in Great Britain by
BPC Paperbacks Ltd.
Aylesbury, Bucks.

CONTENTS

INTRODUCTION

NOTE: Readers who would prefer not to know the details of the stories beforehand are advised to read this Introduction after the book itself.

The publication of Fyodor Mikhailovich Dostoevsky's first novel, *Poor Folk*, in January 1846 was a most striking literary début. This apparently slight and sentimental exchange of letters between a poor, middle-aged government clerk and the young seamstress he loves saw its author elevated practically overnight from obscurity to literary celebrity. The periodical press received the work with widespread acclaim (although the more conservative newspapers and journals were lukewarm). The poet Nekrasov, in whose almanac *Poor Folk* first appeared, insisted that 'a new Gogol has appeared', referring to the strange prose-poet Nikolai Gogol (1809–52), whose grotesque masterpieces are among the finest achievements of nineteenth-century Russian prose; and the leading literary critic of the time and the rallying point for progressive opinion in Russia, Vissarion Belinsky (1811–48), recognizing at once Dostoevsky's promise, summoned him to his presence and told him to his face that he would be a great writer.

The reader who approaches *Poor Folk* today will perhaps wonder what the fuss was about, but it is important to recognize that Dostoevsky's novel, with its implicit affirmation of the humanity and value of even the lowest person and its delicate exploration of the complex psychological effects wrought by poverty and wounded self-esteem, carried the hopes of progressive intellectuals like Belinsky, who saw in emergent Russian literature a 'Natural School' of social realism imbued with humanitarian compassion and civic responsibility—a powerful weapon in the struggle for social reform. For Belinsky the naïve and sentimental hero of *Poor Folk*, Makar Devushkin, articulated the pain of the whole of Russia's underclass of the humiliated and the wronged.

Dostoevsky's success with *Poor Folk* was, however, short-lived. His second novel, *The Double*, also published in 1846, received a frosty reception, and by the time of his arrest and imprisonment for conspiracy in 1849 his reputation was in decline. Even Belinsky reacted with growing suspicion, and eventually hostility, to a string of works in which the humanitarianism and social significance he had so admired in *Poor Folk* were submerged in Dostoevsky's increasing preoccupation with abnormal psychology and grotesquely disordered character types. The writer himself sensed the need for a change of direction as early as October 1846, when he wrote to his brother Mikhail announcing his decision to discontinue work on 'The Shaved Whiskers', another tale dealing with a lowly civil servant lost in the bureaucratic hierarchy of the St Petersburg civil service:

I have abandoned everything, for all this is nothing more than a repetition of old ideas which I have long ago expressed. Now I am compelled to put more original, lively and lucid ideas on to paper. When I had finished 'The Shaved Whiskers' all this became clear to me. In my position uniformity means ruin.

In works such as *The Double* and *Mister Prokharchin* (also 1846) Dostoevsky had employed the figure of the lowly civil servant in order to explore the extreme and sometimes perverse psychological distress experienced by the individual who seeks to assert his independence and individuality within the circumscribed identity allocated to him by society. This had not always succeeded, since the hero's limited imagination and lack of understanding of the forces at work in his own being had inhibited the reader's own comprehension and willingness to share the texture of the character's inner world. The hero's psychological confusion in, for example, *The Double* was reflected in a narrative confusion that rendered the novel tedious and incomprehensible to many of its readers. Dostoevsky's letter to Mikhail signals his intention to adopt a new kind of hero, the 'gentleman-dreamer', socially and intellectually superior to the earlier characters, capable of greater introspection, endowed with a richer imaginative capacity, but hopelessly alienated from reality. If

Devushkin had been the hapless victim of reality, the dreamer was to be fugitive from it.

The choice of such a new hero is not as fortuitous as it might seem: the young Dostoevsky knew only too well the seductive power of romantic dreaming. He too had been a dreamer, and as a student at the St Petersburg Academy of Military Engineering he had conceived a consuming passion for German Romanticism and the works of Friedrich Schiller. This and a sentimental friendship with an unworldly Romantic poet, Ivan Shidlovsky, had facilitated Dostoevsky's withdrawal from real life into a gossamer world of the Romantic imagination. Subsequently the down-to-earth authenticity of *Poor Folk* and its author's growing admiration for the great European social realists like Balzac, Dickens, and George Sand had marked a turn in Dostoevsky's own personal development: a retreat from bootless idealism and a dawning awareness of the problems of the real world. Dostoevsky's own discovery of reality had taught him that the dreamer absorbed in his dreams had 'blunted his talent for real life' and had embarked on a path leading to illusion, solipsism, and spiritual disintegration. A comment of 1847 to the effect that man must 'realize, fulfil and justify his Self in real life' discloses not only the zeal of a reformed dreamer, but also Dostoevsky's recognition of the tragedy of the individual who has sacrificed to abstraction all sense of living life. It is precisely this tragedy that is to be fully explored in Dostoevsky's later novels, in characters such as Raskolnikov in *Crime and Punishment* (1866), who murders a fellow human being for the sake of a theory; in Ivan Karamazov in *The Karamazov Brothers* (1880), whose imaginative constructs compel him to reject life; and in the hero of *Notes from the Underground* (1864), who is reduced to inertia and non-being by a paralysing introspection.

The tragedy of the dreamer lies in his inability to establish a balanced relationship between the external world of reality and the inner world of fantasy, as Dostoevsky explained to his brother in a letter of early 1847: 'The *exterior* must keep in steady balance with the *interior*. Otherwise, in the absence of exterior phenomena, the interior will assume too dangerous an upper hand. Nerves and fantasy will occupy a very large place in one's being.' That Dostoevsky considered the dreamer to be a signicant social phenomenon is indicated not only by the author's adoption of this type as his new hero, but also by an article he published in the *St Petersburg Gazette* in June 1847. In this piece Dostoevsky ironically draws attention to the dreamer as a characteristic Petersburg type, entirely in tune with a city that seemed to the author to encourage withdrawal and alienation and which the hero of *Notes from the Underground* was later to describe as 'the most abstract and premeditated city on earth':

Do you know, ladies and gentlemen, what a dreamer is? It is a Petersburg nightmare, it is sin incarnate, it is a tragedy ... They [the dreamers] usually live in complete solitude, in some inaccessible quarters, as though they were hiding from people and the world, and, generally, there is something melodramatic about them at first sight. They are gloomy and taciturn with their own people, they are absorbed in themselves and are very fond of anything that does not require any effort, anything light and contemplative, everything that has a tender effect on their feelings or excites their sensations. They are fond of reading and they read all sorts of books, even serious scientific books, but they usually lay the book down after reading two or three pages, for they feel completely satisfied. Their imagination, mobile, volatile, light, is already excited, their senses are attuned, and a whole dream-like world, with its joys and sorrows, with its heaven and hell, its ravishing women, heroic deeds ... suddenly possesses the entire being of the dreamer ... Sometimes whole nights pass unnoticed in undescribed joys; sometimes a paradise of love or a whole lifetime ... is experienced in a few hours ... The moments of sobering up are terrible; the poor unfortunate cannot bear them and he immediately takes more of his poison in new increased doses.

Towards the end of his article Dostoevsky comments on the true dangers of such dreaming:

Little by little our curious fellow begins to withdraw from crowds, from common interests, and gradually and imperceptibly he begins to blunt his talent for real life. It begins to seem natural to him that the pleasures attainable through his capricious fantasy are fuller, richer and dearer than life itself. Finally, in his delusion he completely loses that moral sense through which man is capable of appreciating all the beauty of reality. He goes astray, loses himself, lets slip those moments of real happiness; and, in a state of apathy, he folds his arms and does not wish to know that man's life consists in constant contemplation of oneself in nature and in day-to-day reality.

The hero of *White Nights* (1848) is readily identifiable in the picture Dostoevsky draws of the Petersburg dreamer, but the other stories contained in this present volume also illustrate the tragedy that ensues when man loses his sense of 'living life' and sacrifices his being on the altar of abstraction. *White Nights* was not, however, the first of Dostoevsky's artistic works to deal with the theme of the alienated dreamer: the strange tale *The Landlady* (1847) had charted the intellectual disintegration of Ordynov, a solitary young man whose fantasy transforms the grey Petersburg reality into a fairy-tale world populated by beautiful princesses and evil sorcerers. Belinsky was unimpressed by *The Landlady* and dismissed it as 'terrible rubbish', but it is in fact a highly sophisticated artistic structure in which an unstable narrative viewpoint recreates for the reader the same uncertainty experienced by the hero. Dostoevsky was to use the same device again in creating the strange, hallucinatory world of Raskolnikov.

* * *

There is no doubt, though, that Dostoevsky was affected by Belinsky's criticisms of *The Landlady*, and it is possible to see *White Nights* as the author's attempt to re-work the theme of the dreamer in a more lucid fashion. Gone from it is the grotesque and threatening atmosphere of the earlier tale, which derived from Ordynov's inability to distinguish fantasy from reality. The greater clarity of mind of the hero/narrator of *White Nights* invests the work with a new sobriety and detachment. Indeed, the world of the dreamer seems at first to be seductively ideal. Freed from the shackles of reality by 'the Goddess of Imagination', he becomes 'the artist of his own life', living out in his relationship with Nastenka a romantic and sentimental idyll, reinforced by the magic of the early summer white nights when the sun never sets on the beauty of the northern city. The atmosphere of the tale is poetic, lyrical, and immensely touching. It is a hymn sung in praise of youth, springtime, and love, all of which have the power to transfigure mundane reality:

It was a wonderful night, the sort of night that can only occur when we are young, dear reader. The sky was so starry and bright, that one glance was enough to make you ask yourself: surely, ill-natured and peevish people can't possibly exist under a sky like that, can they? That's a young person's question too, dear reader, very much so, but may the good Lord visit it upon you ever and anon!

(p. 3)

It seems that in the unabashed lyricism of *White Nights* and its hero Dostoevsky has distilled all the beauty of his own youthful Romantic idealism, of which he later wrote: 'What did I not dream about in my youth . . . In my whole life there have been no fuller, holier and purer moments than those.' Here Dostoevsky recognizes the enormous *aesthetic* value of such idealistic dreaming. And, as an artist, so he must, for such creative meditation is the crucible in which artistic creation itself is forged. But there is a heavy price to be paid for such uncritical adoration of 'the Goddess of Imagination': the possibility of a wasted life and eventual disillusionment. Dostoevsky had paid some of this price himself, as he admitted when describing his earlier life in an essay of 1861: 'I fell into such a reverie that I overlooked the whole of my youth.'

Despite Konstantin Mochulsky's assertion in his biography of Dostoevsky that 'there is nothing stale or musty' in the image of the young dreamer of *White Nights*, Dostoevsky does use this figure to express his own ambiguous attitude to Romantic idealism. As has been suggested earlier, what distinguishes this dreamer from Ordynov in *The Landlady* is his clarity of vision and ability to regard himself and his existence dispassionately. One of the striking features of his confession to Nastenka, when he describes his life of isolated fantasy, is his tendency to speak of himself *in the third person*.

'No, Nastenka, what is there, what can there be for an indolent sensualist like him in the sort of life that you and I so long for? It is

an impoverished, pitiable existence, so he thinks, failing to foresee
that for him too, perhaps, the dismal hour will strike when he would
exchange all his fantasy-ridden years for one day of this pitiable
life . . .'

(p. 22)

Such detachment clearly reveals the hero's dilemma: hopelessly alienated from and afraid of life, he retreats into
dreams; but he acknowledges the tenuousness of such
dreams, which sooner or later must fade in the face of the
implacable reality of life itself:

'And now I know more than ever that I have squandered all my best
years! I realize that now . . . Now, as I sit next to you and talk
with you, I feel positively terrified of the future, because in that
future loneliness lurks once more, again that musty, pointless
existence.

(p. 25)

'Look, you tell yourself, look how cold the world is becoming. The
years will pass and after them will come grim loneliness, and old
age, quaking on its stick, and after them misery and despair. Your
fantasy world will grow pale, your dreams will fade and die, falling
away like the yellow leaves from the trees . . .'

(p. 27)

The apparent idyll of *White Nights* is an illusion. Beneath the
dreamer's Romantic idealism there already lurks suppressed
despair and the spectre of the Underground, that twilight
zone between fact and fiction where the hero of *Notes from
the Underground* is to carve out his sterile existence of
perverted idealism some fifteen or so years later. *White Nights*
ends on a prophetic note: on returning to his room after
losing Nastenka to his rival, the dreamer experiences a
strange hallucination:

I glanced at Matryona [the maid] . . . She was still a sprightly, *young*
old woman, but I don't know why, she suddenly seemed to me
stooped and decrepit, her eyes dimmed, her face wrinkled . . . I
don't know why, but my room had aged just like the old woman.
The walls and floor had faded, everything had grown dingy; there
were more cobwebs than ever. I don't know why, but when I glanced
out of the window, it seemed that the house opposite had also grown
decrepit and dingy, the stucco on the columns peeling and dropping

off, the cornices darkened and cracked, the dark-ochre walls patchy and mottled . . .

Either a darting ray of sunshine had suddenly vanished behind a rain-cloud and rendered everything dull before my eyes; or perhaps, the entire perspective of my future had flashed before me, so miserable and uninviting, and I saw myself just as I was now, fifteen years on, growing old, in the same room, alone as now with the same old Matryona, grown not a whit more intelligent over the years.

(pp. 55–6)

This 'time warp', by means of which the hero is carried fifteen years into an uninviting future, establishes the relationship of the dreamer of the 1840s to that later grotesquely disillusioned dreamer, the Underground Man, and thus to the heroes of Dostoevsky's mature works. But *White Nights* is linked to the themes of the later works, including the other works in the present volume, in yet another way. It was conceived and written at a time when Dostoevsky was attending meetings of the Petrashevsky Circle, a group of political idealists who met to discuss the ideas of the European utopian socialists. Paramount among such ideas was the dream of a future social order erected upon the ideal of the brotherhood of man. It is difficult to judge whether Dostoevsky shared the political utopianism of the Petrashevsky Circle or was drawn into the conspiracy through naïvety. What is certain is that by the time he returned from imprisonment and exile he was an implacable opponent of all political idealism and all utopian systems that promised to deliver paradise on earth. His Siberian experiences among the criminal classes had convinced him that man's nature was not capable of brotherhood, and that a future secular Golden Age erected on humanism and fraternity was an illusion, albeit a seductive one. As he later remarked in *Winter Notes on Summer Impressions* (1863): 'you only need the finest filament to fall into the machine, and everything at once cracks and falls to pieces. . . . In order to make hare stew, you must first have a hare. But we don't have the hare; that is, we don't have a nature capable of brotherhood.' The Dostoevsky who returned from Siberia in December 1859 was a devout

Orthodox Christian, convinced of the powerlessness of utopian idealism in the face of human evil. Salvation was to be
erected not on the basis of humanism or a transformed
political order, but on the religious rebirth of the individual.

That the sort of utopianism he had encountered at Petrashevsky's was linked to the naïve and sentimental idealism of
the Petersburg dreamer is clarified by Dostoevsky in a
passage in *White Nights* when Nastenka appears to flirt with
the illusion of the brotherhood of man. Moved by sentiment,
she cries out to the dreamer: 'but, you know what crossed my
mind just now? I won't talk about that now, though, just, you
know, in general; it's been in my mind for a long time. Listen,
why can't we all behave like brothers to one another? Why
does even the best of men always keep something back,
something unspoken from the other?' Her subsequent unwit-
ting destruction of the dreamer's hopes of happiness, when
she leaves him for her lover, betrays the naïvety of such
idealism, which overlooks the egoism, sensualism, and will to
power that drive human behaviour. Dostoevsky recognized
that in this imperfect world human relations are based not on
mutual love, but on the clash of egos. This truth was to be
revealed in his later works, and nowhere more emphatically
than in the second story in this volume, *A Gentle Creature*.

*   *   *

A Gentle Creature was first published as the November issue
of Dostoevsky's *Diary of a Writer* for 1876, and the author's
preface to the tale contains an apology for this change to the
Diary's format. Dostoevsky had begun his *Diary of a Writer* in
1873 when he was editor of the reactionary periodical *The
Citizen*, and he took it up again in 1876, long after he had
broken off relations with that periodical. Publication continued intermittently right up until the author's death in early
1881. The *Diary* is a unique literary achievement, and a very
important one in Dostoevsky's œuvre. In one sense, it is a
continuation of those *feuilletons* he wrote in the 1840s and
1860s, in which the figure of the dreamer was first intro-
duced. In another, it is a uniquely candid revelation of the
author's own personality and views on a wide variety of

contemporary issues at a time when he was engaged in the
writing of some of his greatest novels. Finally, the deliberately
provisional and off-the-cuff nature of the work gives us an
intimate glimpse into Dostoevsky's creative processes: it is
the workshop in which *The Karamazov Brothers* was wrought.

   In previous entries in the *Diary* Dostoevsky had been much
exercised by what he considered to be an epidemic of suicides
amongst Russians, including that of the daughter of the great
Russian socialist Alexander Herzen. For Dostoevsky such
suicides were extreme symptoms of a loss of meaning and
spiritual bankruptcy in contemporary life. 'The Russian land
seems to have lost the force to hold people on it', he wrote.
'The so-called life force, the vital feeling of being, without
which no society can exist and the land is liable to fall, is
decidedly disappearing.' Central to the loss of meaning in
contemporary society was the erosion of religious belief;
modern scientific rationalism and materialism had based
existence on a narrow positivism and stripped away the rich
mysteries of the spirit. Herzen's daughter, infected by her
father's lack of spiritual faith, had, according to Dostoevsky,
been crushed by the 'rectilinearity of phenomena' which
reduced life to 'cold darkness and boredom'. It was not,
however, the suicide of Herzen's daughter that provided the
immediate inspiration for *A Gentle Creature*. In the October
1876 issue of the *Diary of a Writer* Dostoevsky had described
a young girl's suicide that had been widely reported in the
press:

A month or so ago all the Petersburg newspapers carried a few brief
lines in small type about a certain Petersburg suicide: a certain poor
young girl, a seamstress, threw herself from a fourth-floor window—
'because she had been quite unable to find work for her livelihood'.
The reports went on to say that she jumped out and fell to the
ground *holding in her hands an icon*. This icon in the hands is a
strange and unheard-of feature in a suicide! This is a sort of meek,
humble suicide. It would appear that there was no fuss or reproach
here: it simply became impossible to go on living; 'God did not wish
it'—and she died, having said her prayers. There are certain things,
no matter how *simple* they seem at first, that you cannot get out of

your mind for a long time, they somehow come to you in your dream, and it is even as though you yourself are to blame for them. This meek soul that destroyed itself involuntarily torments one's thoughts.

This image of a meek 'Petersburg' suicide fused with Dostoevsky's fears about the spiritual bankruptcy of contemporary life to produce an artistic work of great psychological and philosophical depth. Yet the young suicide with an icon in her hands plays a secondary role in Dostoevsky's tale: the focus of interest is on her partner, the introverted and malignant pawnbroker, whose halting narrative represents a desperate attempt to rationalize events and to understand his own role in them. *A Gentle Creature* and its pawnbroker hero are intimately related to Dostoevsky's earlier works and characters. Firstly, and on his own admission, the pawnbroker is a *dreamer*, a descendant of the alienated hero of *White Nights*. However, all traces of the idyllic have been erased from the new hero's life; Romantic idealism has been debased by loneliness and disillusionment into a perverse and destructive spite. As Mochulsky remarks in his biography, 'his traits are long familiar to us: *this is Dostoevsky's eternal companion: the man from underground*'; the pawnbroker's disappointment in life has led to his complete withdrawal, and from the solitude of his soul he draws the resolve to avenge himself on life and to tyrannize those who are weaker than he. The dreamer's sentimental and selfless love for Nastenka in *White Nights* is here corrupted into the spiteful and cruel subjugation of the 'gentle creature'. The irony is, of course, that the young heroine is far from being the meek soul the title implies; she is a proud and spirited creature, as her advertisements for work reveal. The combination of such spirit with her financial and social vulnerability is precisely what attracts the diabolical and despotic pawnbroker:

I was already beginning to look on her as *mine* and had no doubts about my power. You know, that's a really sensual feeling, when you have no doubts at all.

(p. 66)

I'm fond of proud little girls. The proud ones are especially nice when . . . well, when you're confident of your power over them, eh?

(p. 70)

The reader familiar with *Notes from the Underground* will recognize here the same despotism and will to power that drive the Underground Man in his seduction of the prostitute Liza. Surprisingly perhaps, both the pawnbroker and his predecessor entertain the thought that they might actually *love* their victims, but for such monsters love and tyranny are inseparable. The confusion of love with tyranny and despotism is also to be found in the relationship between Rogozhin and Nastasya Filippovna in *The Idiot*, and in this respect it is interesting that the earliest recognizable draft for *A Gentle Creature* may be found in Dostoevsky's notebook for 1869, when he was engaged in work on *The Idiot*. The pride that drives the young girl into a destructive relationship with the pawnbroker is the same pride that draws Nastasya Filippovna to her death by Rogozhin's hand.

But the links that bind *A Gentle Creature* to *The Idiot* are not confined to the repetition in the former of psychological motifs and character relationships from the latter. Both works are erected on the same philosophical premiss: that the contemporary age is a spiritual wilderness, a desert of will and moral solitude in which man has lost all sense of direction and purpose. In *The Idiot* the minor character Lebedev, an interpreter of the Apocalypse, launches an attack on the spiritual vacuum at the heart of contemporary life that is recognizably Dostoevsky's own: 'the whole thing, sir, altogether accursed, the entire spirit of these last centuries, in its scientific and practical totality, is perhaps really accursed, sir'. In Lebedev's analysis, modern man, driven by egoism and self-interest and having lost the capacity for love and compassion, has destroyed the very basis of his existence. Lebedev tells of a twelfth-century monk who, after twenty years of cannibalism, confessed and went to the stake. What was it, he asks, that drove him to confession and expiation?

'There must have been something stronger than the stake, the fire, even the habit of twenty years! There must have been an idea more powerful than any disaster, famine, torture, plague, leprosy, and all that hell which mankind could not have borne without that one binding idea which directed men's minds and fertilized the springs of life! Show me anything resembling that power in our age. . . . Show me a force which binds today's humanity together with half the power it possessed in those centuries. . . .'

Lebedev then proceeds to invest his diagnosis with an apocalyptic colouring:

'we're in the time of the third horse, the black one, the one that has the rider with scales in his hand, because in our age everything is weighed in the balance and settled by agreement, and all men seek only their own due: 'one measure of wheat for one denarius and three measures of barley for one denarius' . . . as well as wanting to have freedom of spirit, a pure heart and a sound body, and all God's gifts added thereunto. But they cannot have these things by right alone, and the pale horse will follow and he whose name is Death, and after him, Hell . . .'

Lebedev's remarks in *The Idiot* provide the frame into which we must set the pawnbroker's terrible vision of spiritual desolation at the end of *A Gentle Creature*:

Inertia . . . Oh, nature! People on earth are alone, that is the calamity of it! 'Is anyone alive on the plain?' shouts the old Russian hero, and no one responds. I am no epic hero, but I too shout, and no one responds. They say the sun animates the universe. The sun will rise and look at it—is it not a corpse? Everything is dead and corpses are everywhere. Only people exist and around them is silence—that is what the earth is! 'People, love one another!' Who said that? Whose behest is that? The pendulum ticks on, insensible, horrible.

(p. 103)

But in the midst of this terrible desolation—the most terrible passage, perhaps, in the whole of Dostoevsky's art—a voice in the wilderness urges human contact and mutual love. Yet in this plea we do not hear the naïve idealism of Nastenka as she reaches for the mirage of brotherhood on earth. The voice that interrupts the pawnbroker's moral despair is the voice of God, urging love for one's fellow man not as some short cut to a secular utopia, the re-establishment of paradise on earth, but as the first and necessary step in the spiritual rebirth of an individual human soul, who through contrition and suffering will find his own way to salvation.

A Gentle Creature is clearly structured on two artistic devices: the use of interior monologue to express the pawn-broker's approach to the truth, and the motif of the duel. Both reflect the tale's central philosophical and religious design. Dostoevsky apologizes for his improbable and 'fantas-tic' narrative form in his preface to the tale, but the fluid and provisional flow of interior monologue—with its hesitant syntax, pauses, ellipses, and sudden moments of epiphany—creates great emotional intensity and immediacy. It also, as Robert Jackson observes in his *Art of Dostoevsky*, expresses the work's central theme—solitude. The pawnbroker, silent and unyielding with his wife, speaks only to himself. The words that could have brought him and his wife together cannot escape the confines of his own enclosed conscious-ness; tragedy comes about through the absence of dialogue. In the relationship between the pawnbroker and the gentle creature dialogue is replaced by duelling. In the emotional and psychological duel he fights with his wife the hero seeks to justify himself in his own and her eyes for the duel he failed to fight as an army officer. The terrible bedroom episode when he closes his eyes in the face of his wife's revolver is central here: 'That calamity had occurred just at the right time. In withstanding the revolver, I had avenged all my grim past history. And although no one knew of it, *she* did, and that was all that mattered to me . . .' The pawnbro-ker's willingness to gamble all on the outcome of a duel of wills, to risk death for the sake of asserting his power over another, forges a link between this tale and Dostoevsky's earlier novel *The Gambler* (1866). Both gambling and duelling betray the tragedy of contemporary alienated man, trapped in the wastes of unbelief and determined to take on a universe governed not by meaning, but by the blind laws of chance.

*   *   *

The final story in this volume, *The Dream of a Ridiculous Man*, is in many respects a pendant to *A Gentle Creature*. It too first appeared in the *Diary of a Writer*, in the April issue for 1877, and it too carries the subtitle 'A Fantastic Story'. On this occasion, though, the description 'fantastic' applies not to the work's narrative form, but to its apparently utopian content—the hero's dream of a Golden Age where men live together in a state of natural harmony and brotherly love. The Ridiculous Man himself is the same sort of alienated dreamer as the pawnbroker, aware of his oddness and unable to relate to the community, 'a modern progressive and vile Petersburger'. He represents the tragic end of the road for the Petersburg dreamer: so complete is his introspection and estrangement, that he doubts the reality of the world about him. The ego, long deprived of social intercourse, floats in a vacuum where the only certainty is that of its own inviolability and isolation:

I have unaccountably grown somewhat calmer. . . . Perhaps it was because a terrible anguish had developed within my soul, occasioned by . . . the dawning conviction that in the world at large, *nothing mattered*. . . . All of a sudden, I realized that it *would not matter* to me whether the world existed or whether there was nothing at all anywhere. I begin to intuit and sense with all my being, that *there was nothing around me.*

(p. 108)

For the Ridiculous Man intellectualism, egoism, and withdrawal from life have resulted in spiritual death, moral indifference, and the sort of solipsistic non-being anticipated by the pawnbroker at the very end of *A Gentle Creature*. The act of suicide presents itself to him as a logical way out of the tedium and tyranny of a meaningless universe. On a cold, damp, and unutterably gloomy November night, when St Petersburg seems merely an externalization of the darkness in his soul, he resolves to shoot himself. But his resolve is weakened by the memory of a suffering little girl whom he has abandoned in the street—the grain of compassion and human sympathy is sown in his soul. In his dream he does shoot himself, not in the head, as he had always planned, but in the heart—a tacit acknowledgement, perhaps, of the beginning of spiritual rebirth; his heart is no longer empty. The dream that follows is one familiar to readers of

Dostoevsky's novels of the 1870s: it is that same vision of a
Golden Age at the dawn of man's existence, suffused with
warm Mediterranean sunlight, that had come to Stavrogin in
Devils (1872) and Versilov in *An Accidental Family* (*A Raw
Youth*) (1875). In reality Dostoevsky acquired the image from
a painting by Claude Lorrain, *Acis and Galatea*, which he had
seen at the Dresden picture gallery in 1867. Stavrogin, too,
refers to this same painting, which he relates to his own
tormented, elusive dreams of paradise on earth, and his
response to it is undoubtedly similar to Dostoevsky's own:

In a gallery in Dresden there's a painting by Claude Lorrain, called
I believe in the catalogue 'Acis and Galatea', although I've always
referred to it as 'The Golden Age', I don't know why. I'd seen it
before, but just about three days earlier I'd noticed it once again in
passing. It was this picture that appeared to me in my dream, not as
a picture, but as if it were the real thing.

It was some little place in the Greek archipelago; there were
gentle blue waves, islands and cliffs, a luxuriant shore, a fantastic
panorama in the distance, a beckoning, setting sun—beyond
description. One was reminded of the cradle of European civiliza-
tion, the first scenes of mythology, of the earthly paradise. . . . What
a splendid race lived here! They woke up and fell asleep happy and
innocent; the groves were filled with their merry songs; their
abundant, untiring energy went into love and simple joys. The sun
flooded the islands and sea with its rays, taking delight in its
beautiful children. A wonderful dream, a lofty delusion! The most
improbable fantasy ever conceived, to which all mankind has devoted
its strength throughout its life, for which it's sacrificed everything,
for which men have died on the cross and prophets have been killed,
without which people do not wish to live but are unable even to die.
I seemed to experience all these sensations in this dream; I don't
know what it was that I dreamt precisely, but the cliffs and sea, the
slanted rays of the setting sun—all this I still seemed to see, when I
woke up and opened my eyes, for the first time in my life literally
awash with tears.

The development of these same details, drawn from Dostoevsky's contemplation of Claude's painting, in the dream of
the Ridiculous Man has led Mochulsky to conclude that the
Dream, 'wondrous and unique in its genre, brilliantly culmi-
nates Dostoevsky's utopian conceptions'. But this overlooks

the fact that *The Dream of a Ridiculous Man* is not a utopian work. Its hero's vision is not primarily a prophetic glimpse of some future paradise on earth; it is, if anything, a retrospective vision from Genesis, a recapitulation of the Fall of Man and his exclusion from paradise. The hero brings with him the seeds of corruption, and in their subsequent fall from grace the innocents of his dream relive the whole degrading process of human history. They discover debauchery, violence, enmity, isolation, war, and egoism; they discover the 'insights' of reason and analysis, but they lose the harmony they once enjoyed with themselves and with nature; they discover the Dostoevskian delights of cruelty and self-abasement, of tyranny and pride; they even discover, as they contemplate the ruins of the world they have defiled, the allure of socialism and utopianism, as they dream of restoring order to the chaos about them. What we witness in this tale is the destruction of paradise.

The dream of the Golden Age remained for Dostoevsky an image of great aesthetic force; but for him, as for Stavrogin, it was 'a lofty delusion, the most improbable fantasy ever conceived'. It was not capable of being translated into reality by any of man's rational insights, scientific advances, or political and economic systems. The dream provides the Ridiculous Man with an image of perfection, but it is the discovery of compassion in his heart for a suffering child that suggests the possibility of his personal salvation, as it does for Dmitry in *The Karamazov Brothers*. *The Dream of a Ridiculous Man* deals with religious beginnings, not utopian endings; it is not about the realization of earthly paradise and the brotherhood of man, but how the seed of love planted in an individual heart can allow that man to embark upon the painful path that leads first to Calvary and then to resurrection.

W. J. LEATHERBARROW

SELECT BIBLIOGRAPHY

CATTEAU, JACQUES, *Dostoyevsky and the Process of Literary Creation*, trans. Audrey Littlewood (Cambridge, 1989).

FANGER, DONALD, *Dostoevsky and Romantic Realism* (Chicago, 1967).

FRANK, JOSEPH, *Dostoevsky: The Seeds of Revolt 1821–1849* (Princeton and London, 1976).

—— *Dostoevsky: The Years of Ordeal 1850–1859* (Princeton and London, 1983).

—— *Dostoevsky: The Stir of Liberation 1860–1865* (Princeton and London, 1986).

JACKSON, ROBERT LOUIS, *The Art of Dostoevsky: Deliriums and Nocturnes* (Princeton, 1981).

JONGE, ALEX DE, *Dostoevsky and the Age of Intensity* (London, 1975).

KJETSAA, GEIR, *Fyodor Dostoyevsky: A Writer's Life* (London, 1988).

LEATHERBARROW, W. J., *Fedor Dostoevsky: A Reference Guide* (Boston, Mass., 1990).

MOCHULSKY, KONSTANTIN, *Dostoevsky: His Life and Work*, trans. Michael Minihan (Princeton, 1967).

WASIOLEK, EDWARD, *Dostoevsky: The Major Fiction* (Cambridge, Mass., 1964).

CHRONOLOGY OF FYODOR DOSTOEVSKY

Italicized items are works by Dostoevsky listed by year of first publication. Dates are Old Style, which means that they lag behind those used in nineteenth-century western Europe by twelve days.

1821	Fyodor Mikhailovich Dostoevsky is born in Moscow, the son of an army doctor (30 October).
1837	His mother dies.
1838	Enters the Engineering Academy in St Petersburg as an army cadet.
1839	His father dies, possibly murdered by his serfs.
1842	Is promoted Second Lieutenant.
1843	Translates Balzac's *Eugénie Grandet*.
1844	Resigns his army commission.
1846	*Poor Folk* *The Double* *Mister Prokharchin*
1847	*The Landlady*
1848	*White Nights*
1849	*Netochka Nezvanova* Is led out for execution in the Semenovsky Square in St Petersburg (22 December); his sentence is commuted at the last moment to penal servitude, to be followed by army service and exile, in Siberia.
1850–4	Serves four years at the prison at Omsk in western Siberia.
1854	Is released from prison (March), but is immediately posted as a private soldier to an infantry battalion stationed at Semipalatinsk, in western Siberia.
1855	Is promoted Corporal. Death of Nicholas I; accession of Alexander II.
1856	Is promoted Ensign.
1857	Marries Maria Dmitrievna Isaeva (6 February).
1859	Resigns his army commission with the rank of Second Lieutenant (March), and receives permission to return to European Russia. Resides in Tver (August–December). Moves to St Petersburg (December).

Uncle's Dream
Stepanchikovo Village

1861   Begins publication of a new literary monthly, *Vremia*,
         founded by himself and his brother Mikhail (January).
         The Emancipation of the Serfs.
         The Insulted and the Injured
         A Series of Essays on Literature

1861–2   *Memoirs from the House of the Dead*

1862   His first visit to western Europe, including England and
         France.

1863   *Winter Notes on Summer Impressions*
         Vremia is closed by the authorities for political reasons.

1864   Launches a second journal, *Epokha* (March).
         His first wife dies (15 April).
         His brother Mikhail dies (10 July).
         Notes from the Underground.

1865   *Epokha* collapses for financial reasons (June).

1866   Attempted assassination of Alexander II by Dmitry Kara-
         kozov (April).
         Crime and Punishment
         The Gambler

1867   Marries Anna Grigorevna Snitkina, his stenographer, as
         his second wife (15 February)
         Dostoevsky and his bride leave for western Europe
         (April).

1867–71 The Dostoevskys reside abroad, chiefly in Dresden, but
         also in Geneva, Vevey, Florence, and elsewhere.

1868   *The Idiot*

1870   *The Eternal Husband*

1871   The Dostoevskys return to St Petersburg. Birth of their
         first son, Fyodor (16 July).

1871–2   *Devils* (also called *The Possessed*)

1873–4   Edits the weekly journal *Grazhdanin*.

1873–81 *Diary of a Writer*

1875   *An Accidental Family* (*A Raw Youth*)

1876   *A Gentle Creature*; first published in *Diary of a Writer*.

1877   *The Dream of a Ridiculous Man*; first published in *Diary of
         a Writer*.

1878   Death of Dostoevsky's beloved three-year-old son
         Alesha (16 May).

1879–80 *The Karamazov Brothers*

1880   His speech at lavish celebrations held in Moscow in honour of Pushkin is received with frenetic enthusiasm on 8 June, and marks the high point of his reputation during his lifetime.

1881   Dostoevsky dies in St Petersburg (28 January).
        Alexander II is assassinated (1 March).

WHITE NIGHTS

WHITE NIGHTS

WHITE NIGHTS

A SENTIMENTAL NOVEL

(From the Memoirs of a Dreamer)

> Or was he fated from the start,
> to live for just one fleeting instant
> within the purlieus of your heart?*
>
> Ivan Turgenev

THE FIRST NIGHT

IT was a wonderful night, the sort of night that can only occur when we are young, dear reader. The sky was so starry and bright, that one glance was enough to make you ask yourself: surely, ill-natured and peevish people can't possibly exist under a sky like that, can they? That's a young person's question too, dear reader, very much so, but may the good Lord visit it upon you ever and anon! . . . Speaking of sundry peevish and ill-natured gentlemen, I couldn't help recalling my own impeccable behaviour over the whole of that day. From first thing that morning, I had been tormented by a singular feeling of despondency. All of a sudden, I had started to imagine that everyone was abandoning me, steering clear of me, solitary fellow that I am. Of course, you may well ask: who on earth was this 'everyone', since by then I had been living in Petersburg for eight years and had barely managed to make a single acquaintance. Still, what need had I of acquaintances? I was acquainted with all Petersburg in any event; that was why I imagined I was being abandoned when all Petersburg abruptly packed up and left for the country. I felt terrified of being left on my own, and drifted about the city for three days on end in a state of profound misery, without the least notion of what was the matter with me. Whether I went to Nevsky Prospect, or the Summer

Garden or wandered along the embankment—not a single face among all those I had got used to encountering there at a given time in the course of the year. They don't know me, of course, but I certainly know them. I know them intimately; I have come to know their every expression—I feast my eyes when they are cheerful and feel downcast when they are sad. I have practically struck up a friendship with the old fellow I meet every blessed day, at a certain time, by the Fontanka Canal. Such a grave, thoughtful countenance he has, perpetually whispering to himself as he brandishes his left arm. In his other hand, he carries a gold-toppped cane, long and knotty. He's actually become aware of me and takes a cordial interest. If I did not happen to be at that spot at the appropriate time, I am convinced he would mope. For this reason we sometimes almost greet one another, especially when we are both in good humour. Not long ago, when we hadn't seen each other for all of two days, and met on the third, we were on the point of snatching at our hats, but happily bethought ourselves in time, let our hands fall, and passed by one another with all solicitude.

The very houses are known to me. When I am walking along, each of them seems to slip out into the street ahead and look at me, all windows, as if to say: 'Good day; how are you keeping? I'm quite well for my part, praise be, in fact I'm having a new storey added in May.' Or: 'How are you? I'm having repairs done tomorrow.' Or again: 'I almost burned down, what a fright I got!' and so on. I have my favourites among them, indeed intimate friends; one of them intends to have treatment from an architect this summer. I'll make a point of dropping by every day to make sure he doesn't overdo things, Lord preserve it ... I'll never forget what happened to one ever so pretty rose-pink cottage. It was such a sweet little stone cottage and it looked so benignly at me and so proudly at its ungainly neighbours, that my heart positively rejoiced whenever I chanced to pass by. Then all of a sudden, last week, as I was walking along the street and glancing over at my friend, I heard a plaintive cry: 'They're painting me yellow!' Villains! Barbarians! They spared nothing, neither column nor cornice, and my friend turned as yellow as a canary. The incident fairly sickened me and ever since then I've not felt up to seeing my poor, disfigured friend, now painted the colour of the celestial empire.*

So now you understand, dear reader, in what way I am acquainted with all Petersburg.

I have said already that I was tormented by anxiety for all of three days until I divined what was causing it. I felt on edge out of doors (this and that person was absent, where had so-and-so gone?) nor was I myself at home. I spent two evenings trying to decide what was amiss in my little nook. Why did I feel so ill at ease there? Baffled, I surveyed my green, smoke-begrimed walls, and the ceiling hung about with the cobwebs Matryona cultivated so successfully. I looked over all my furniture, inspecting every chair, wondering if that was where the trouble lay (because I lose my bearings if so much as a single chair is in a different place from yesterday), then looked out of the window. All in vain . . . it made not an atom of difference. I even took it into my head to summon Matryona, and gave her a fatherly dressing-down on the spot about the cobwebs and her general slovenliness, but she simply gave me an astonished look and went off without a word; so the cobwebs have hung there ever since, safe and sound. It was only this morning that I finally realized what the trouble was. Why of course, they were leaving me and clearing off to their dachas! Do excuse the vulgar parlance, but I was in no mood for lofty phrases . . . after all, every single person in Petersburg had either moved or was in the process of moving to their country villa. In my eyes every worthy man of respectable appearance hiring a cab, at once became transformed into a worthy paterfamilias, travelling unencumbered after his daily official duties, back to the bosom of his family at the dacha. This was because every passer-by now had a most peculiar air about him, which virtually spoke out loud to anyone he encountered: 'We, gentlemen, are only here in passing, you know, and in two hours' time, we're off to the dacha.' If a window opened, after a preliminary tattoo of little sugar-white fingers, and a pretty girl's head emerged, calling out to a flower-seller, I at once jumped to the conclusion that the reason for purchase was not so as to enjoy the spring and its flowers in a stuffy urban apartment, but that they were all on the point of leaving for their dacha and taking the flowers with them. I had, moreover, developed such expertise in my new and singular mode of enquiry that just by looking at them I could infallibly deduce the sort of dacha they possessed. The denizens of Kamenny or Aptekarsky Islands, or the Peterhof Road, were distinguished by their studied elegance of manner, their fashionable summer dress, and the splendid carriages in which they drove into town. Those who lived in Pargolovo and the more outlying parts struck one immediately with their solid air of worldly wisdom, while the sojourner on Krestovsky Island was notable for an appearance of imperturbable good humour.* If I happened to come across a long procession of carters, walking lazily, reins in hand, alongside waggons piled high with furniture of every kind—tables, chairs, Turkish and non-Turkish sofas, and other domestic goods and chattels, on the very summit of which often presided a skinny cook, guarding the master's goods like the apple of her eye; or if I watched boats heavy-laden with household effects, gliding along the Neva or the Fontanka towards the Black River and the islands—those waggons and boats multiplied tenfold, a hundredfold in my imagination; it seemed as if everything had just upped and left, everything had migrated in whole caravans to the dacha; it seemed as if Petersburg was threatening to turn into a desert, so much so that eventually I began to feel ashamed, and miserably resentful; I had no dacha and no pretext to go to one. I was ready to leave with every load, with every worthy individual of respectable appearance hiring a cab; but absolutely nobody invited me, not one; it was as if they had forgotten me, as if I was actually something alien to them!

I walked a great deal and for long periods at a time, contriving, as was my wont, to become totally oblivious to my surroundings. All of a sudden, I found myself at one of the city gates. On the instant, my spirits rose and I strode through the barrier, taking my way past cultivated fields and meadows. I felt no hint of fatigue, merely sensing with every fibre of my being that a burden was slipping from my mind. All the passers-by regarded me in such an amiable fashion that they actually seemed on the point of greeting me; they were all so pleased about something that to a man they were smoking cigars. And I was glad too in a way I had never been before. It was just as if I had suddenly found myself in Italy, so powerful an effect did the natural scene produce in me, a semi-invalid townee, almost suffocated by being pent within the city.

There is something ineffably touching about our Petersburg countryside when, with the onset of spring, nature suddenly puts forth all her strength, all the power bestowed on her by heaven; she decks heself out in all her finery, gay with flowers ... It puts you in mind of some frail and sickly girl you sometimes note with pity, even a sort of compassionate love—and at others simply fail to notice at all, who suddenly, in an instant, becomes inexplicably, marvellously beautiful, while you, overwhelmed and enraptured, are forced to ask yourself what power has made those sad, pensive eyes glitter with such fire; what power has summoned up the blood to those wan, pinched cheeks; what has infused passion into those gentle features; why is her bosom heaving so; what has suddenly conjured up animation, strength, and beauty in the face of that poor girl, to make it glow with such a smile, and come alive with flashing, sparkling laughter like that? You glance round, filled with surmise, looking for someone ... But the moment has passed and next day perhaps you will encounter once again the same abstracted, brooding glance as before, the same wan face, the same meek and diffident movements; possibly accompanied by a feeling of remorse, traces even of a sort of numb, aching vexation at having been momentarily carried away ... You regret that this fleeting beauty should have faded so swiftly and irrevocably, that it had flashed so beguilingly, so vainly before you— regret that there had been no time for you to fall in love with it ...

Yet all the same, my night was even better than my day! This is what happened.

I got back to the city very late and it had already struck ten by the time I was approaching my apartment. My way led along a canal* embankment where not a living soul is to be encountered at that hour. Of course, I do live in a very far-flung district of the city. I was walking along and singing, because when I'm happy, I always hum something to myself, like any other happy individual who has neither friends nor close acquaintances, and so no one to share his joy in a moment of gladness. All at once, I became caught up in a most unexpected adventure.

Just to one side of me, leaning up against the canal railing, stood a woman; with her elbows pressed against the ironwork, she was evidently staring intently at the turbid waters of the canal. She was wearing the sweetest yellow cap and a fetching little black mantilla. 'She's a young girl and bound to have dark hair', thought I. However, she had seemingly not heard my footsteps and didn't even stir when I walked by with bated breath and thudding heart. 'That's odd', I thought, 'she must be very preoccupied about something'; then I suddenly halted, transfixed. I had caught the sound of muffled weeping. Yes! My ears had not deceived me; the girl was crying and a moment later came more and more sobbing. Good heavens! My heart shrank. I might be shy as far as women were concerned, but at such a moment! ... I turned back and stepped towards her; I would certainly have brought out 'Madam!' had I not been aware that the exclamation had been used a thousand times in every Russian high society novel. That alone prevented me. But while I was searching for words, the girl recollected herself, looked round, realized the situation and, with lowered eyes, slipped past me along the embankment. I at once made to follow, but she divined my intention and, quitting the embankment, crossed the street and set off along the pavement. I did not dare to cross after her. My heart was fluttering like an imprisoned bird. All of a sudden, a chance incident came to my aid.

On the other side of the street, not far from my unknown lady, there suddenly appeared a gentleman in a frock coat. He was of respectable years, but far from respectable gait. He came along, staggering a little and leaning cautiously against the wall. The girl meanwhile was walking as straight as an arrow, swiftly and nervously as all girls do who are disinclined to have anyone volunteering to escort them home at night; of course there was no chance of the swaying gentleman catching her up, had not my muffed attempt prompted him to resort to special measures. Abruptly, without a word to anyone, my gentleman sprang forward and ran as fast as his legs would carry him to catch up with the unknown girl. She was walking along like the wind, but the swaying gentleman drew closer, then overtook her. The girl screamed—and . . . I bless the fates for the excellent knotted stick which chanced to be in my right hand on that occasion. In a flash I found myself on the far side of the street; the unwanted gentleman realized the situation instantly, took cognizance of the irresistible force of reason, and silently dropped back. Only when we were a considerable distance away did he start voicing protestations against me in rather vigorous terms. But his words barely reached us.

'Give me your hand', I said to my mysterious lady, 'and he won't dare pester us again.'

She gave me her hand wordlessly, still shaking with anxiety and alarm. Ah, how I blessed the unwanted gentleman at that moment! I gave her a fleeting glance: I had guessed right, she had dark hair—and was extremely pretty; teardrops still glistened on her dark eyelashes, but whether from her recent fright or her previous grief, I don't know. However, a smile was now playing on her lips. She also took a covert glance at me, flushed slightly, and dropped her eyes.

'There you are, why on earth did you turn me away just now? If I'd been with you nothing would have happened . . .'

'But you were a stranger: I thought you might . . .'

'But you don't know me now, do you?'

'A little bit. Why are you trembling for example?'

'Ah, you've guessed straight away!' I responded, elated that my girl was so perceptive: in a pretty girl that never comes amiss. 'Yes, you guessed immediately the sort of man I am. It's true, I am shy with girls; I'm as nervous as you were a minute ago, when that man frightened you, I won't deny it . . . I'm the one who's full of nerves now. It's just like a dream, and even in dreams I never imagined I would ever be talking with a woman.'

'What? Really?'

'Yes, if my hand is trembling, it's because it's never been held by such a pretty little hand as yours. I've got out of the habit of women; that is to say, I've never been in the habit; I'm on my own, you see . . . I don't so much as know how to talk to them. Even now, I don't know if I've said something idiotic to you. Tell me honestly; I assure you, I won't be offended . . .'

'No, not at all, not at all, quite the contrary. And if you really insist on my being frank, I'll tell you that women like that sort of shyness; and if you want me to go on, it appeals very much to me as well, and I shan't turn you away till we get right to the house.'

'You'll soon make me stop being shy', I began, breathless with rapture, 'and farewell to all my resources! . . .'

'Resources? What resources, what for? Now that's not nice at all.'

'I'm sorry, it won't happen again, it was a slip of the tongue; but at a moment like this you can't expect me not to want to . . .'

'Make a favourable impression, you mean?'

'Well, yes; but do have pity, I implore you. Consider the person I am! Here I am 26 already and I've never seen anybody. How on earth am I supposed to be silver-tongued and say just the right things? In any case, it's in your interest for everything to be open and above board . . . I don't know how to keep quiet when my heart speaks within me. Well, never mind . . . Can you credit it, not one woman, never ever! Not even an acquaintance! It's all I dream about every day, that eventually I'll meet someone, sometime. Ah, if you only knew how many times I've been in love that way! . . .'

'What way do you mean, who on earth with? . . .'

'Oh, nobody, an ideal, the woman I dream about. I invent whole love-affairs in my dreams. Ah, how little you know me! Of course I couldn't help coming across one or two women, but not real women, they were all landladies and that sort of

thing . . . But you'll laugh when I tell you that there have
been times when I thought I would strike up a conversation,
just like that, with some upper-class lady in the street, when
she was unattended, naturally; without presumption of
course, respectfully, with feeling; tell her I was a lost soul on
my own, that she was not to turn me away, that I had no
means of meeting any woman at all; impress upon her that it
was positively a woman's duty not to spurn the humble plea
of an unfortunate like me. That ultimately all I asked was to
hear a word or two of human kindness, a show of concern,
for her not to dismiss me at once, but believe what I was
saying and hear me out, laugh at me if she pleased, inspire
me with hope, just say a word or two, that's all, even if we
never met again! . . . But you're laughing . . . Still, that's why
I'm telling you all this . . .'

'Don't be annoyed; I'm only laughing because you're your
own worst enemy, and if you'd only made the attempt you
might perhaps have succeeded, even in the open street; the
simplest way is always best . . . unless she was silly or
particularly cross about something just at that point, no
decent woman could bring herself to send you away without
those few words you begged for so timidly . . . or no, what am
I saying! Of course she would assume you were some
madman. I was judging by myself. I know a lot about the way
people go on!'

'Oh, thank you!' I exclaimed. 'You've no idea what you've
just done for me!'

'All right now, that's all right. But tell me how you realized
I was the kind of woman with whom . . . well, whom you
considered worthy of . . . consideration and friendship . . . in
a word, not a landlady as you call them. Why did you make
up your mind to approach me?'

'Why? Why? But you were alone and that man was too
audacious—and it's dark: you must agree, it was my bounden
duty . . .'

'No, no, before that, on the other side. You did intend to
speak to me, didn't you?'

'On the other side? I honestly don't know what to say; I'm
afraid . . . You know, I was feeling really happy today, I was

singing as I walked along; I'd been outside the city; I'd never experienced such moments of happiness before. You . . . perhaps I imagined . . . Oh, forgive me for reminding you: I thought you were crying, and I . . . I couldn't bear that . . . my heart shrank within me . . . Heavens! Surely I was allowed to feel sorry for you? Surely it wasn't a sin to feel a human compassion towards you? . . . I'm sorry, I said compassion . . . Well, what I mean is, surely my involuntary impulse to speak to you couldn't have caused you offence? . . .'

'Don't remind me; that's enough, don't go on', said the girl, lowering her eyes and squeezing my hand. 'I'm the one to blame for bringing the subject up; but I'm glad I wasn't mistaken in you . . . still I'm home now; I go this way into the lane; it's only a step . . . Goodbye and thank you . . .'

'Oh but surely, surely we'll meet again? . . . Surely we can't leave it at this?'

'There you are', said the girl, laughing. 'At first you just wanted a few words, and now . . . well, anyway, I'm saying nothing either way . . . Perhaps we will meet again . . .'

'I'll come here tomorrow', I said. 'Oh, do forgive me, I'm starting to insist . . .'

'Yes, you are impatient . . . almost insistent . . .'

'Listen to me, do listen', I broke in. 'Forgive me if I say the wrong thing again . . . But the fact is: I can't stay away tomorrow. I'm a dreamer; I have so little actual life that I regard moments like this one as rare indeed and I can't help repeating them in my dreams. I will dream about you all night, all week, all year. I will come here tomorrow without fail, here to this very spot, at this precise time, and be happy as I recall the events of today. I cherish this place. I have two or three such places in Petersburg already. Once I even began weeping over my memories, like you . . . Who knows, perhaps you too were weeping over your memories ten minutes or so back . . . I'm sorry, I forgot myself again; perhaps you were once particularly happy here.'

'Very well', said the girl. 'I may well come here tomorrow, at ten o'clock as well. I can see that there's no keeping you away . . . The fact is, I have to be here; don't think I'm arranging a rendezvous; I'm letting you know in advance that I have to be here on business of my own. But . . . well I will tell you frankly, then: it will be just as well if you do come; in the first place there may be more unpleasantness like tonight, but leaving that aside . . . what I mean to say is, I just feel like seeing you . . . to say a word or two. But see that you don't think badly of me now—don't go thinking that I arrange meetings just like that . . . I wouldn't even be doing it if . . . But let that be my secret! One proviso in advance . . .'

'Proviso! Go on, tell me, tell me everything in advance; I agree to it all, I'm ready to do anything', I cried ecstatically. 'I can guarantee—I will be respectful and do as you say . . . you know me . . .'

'It's precisely because I do know you that I'm inviting you tomorrow', said the girl, laughing. 'I know you through and through. But see that you observe one condition: above all (just be good enough to do as I ask, I mean what I say, you know), don't fall in love with me . . . You must not do that, believe me. I'm ready to be friends, there's my hand . . . But no falling in love, I beg you!'

'I swear to you', I cried, seizing her little hand . . .

'Come now, don't swear, I'm well aware you're capable of flaring up like gunpowder. Don't think badly of me for speaking like that. If you only knew . . . I have no one to talk with, no one to ask for advice. Of course one doesn't find confidants on the streets, but you're an exception. I know you as if we had been friends for twenty years . . . You won't let me down will you?'

'You'll see . . . but I don't know how I'm going to survive the next twenty-four hours.'

'Get a good night's sleep; good night—and remember that I've already put my faith in you. You came out with something really fine just now: surely one doesn't have to account for every emotion, even human sympathy! You know, that was so well said that the idea of confiding in you came to me at once . . .'

'Of course, but confide what? What is this about?'

'Till tomorrow. Let it remain a secret for the time being.

That will suit you; it will give the thing a touch of romance. I may tell you tomorrow, but perhaps not . . . I'll talk a little bit more with you, we'll get to know each other better . . .'

'Oh, I'll tell you all about myself tomorrow! But what's happening? Really it's as if a miracle were taking place . . . Good lord, where am I? Don't tell me that you're angry with yourself for not turning me away in the first place, as some other woman might have done? Two minutes and you have made me happy for ever. Yes, happy; who can tell, you may have reconciled me with myself, resolved all my doubts . . . Perhaps moments such as these do come upon me . . . Well, I'll tell you all about it tomorrow, you'll find out everything, everything . . .'

'Very well, I accept; you tell first . . .'

'Agreed.'

'*Au revoir*!'

'*Au revoir*!'

And we parted. I walked about all night; I could not bring myself to return home. I was so happy . . . Till tomorrow!

THE SECOND NIGHT

'THERE, you see, you've survived!' she said to me, laughing and taking both my hands.

'I've already been here two hours; you don't know what I've been through all day!'

'I do, I do . . . but let's get on. You know why I've come? Not to talk nonsense like yesterday. From now on, we have to act more sensibly. I thought all this over for ages last night.'

'About what though? Act more sensibly about what? I'm willing enough for my part, but honestly, what's happening now is the most sensible action of my life.'

'Do you really mean that? Well for a start, I beg you not to squeeze my hand so; secondly, I have to announce that I have been devoting a lot of thought to you today.'

'Well, and what was the end result?'

'The end result? That we have to start all over from the beginning, because I decided today that I still don't know you at all; that I acted like a child yesterday, like some little girl, and naturally it transpired that it was all the fault of my good nature, I mean I ended up praising myself as always happens when we start analysing our own actions. So, to rectify my error, I decided to make the most detailed enquiries about you. However, since there's no one to ask about you, you're the one who has to tell me all there is to know. What sort of man are you? Come along now, do make a start and tell me your life story.'

'Life story!' I cried, alarmed. 'Life story! But how do you know I have one? I haven't got a life story . . .'

'So how have you lived without a life story?' she interposed, laughing.

'Without a story of any kind, that's how; as the saying goes, I've kept myself to myself, I mean completely on my own, utterly alone—you understand what that means?'

'But what do you mean—alone? You've never seen anybody ever?'

'Oh no, I see them to set eyes on, but I'm alone just the same.'

'What, you mean you actually don't talk to a soul?'

'Strictly speaking, no I don't.'

'Now just who are you, explain yourself! Wait, I can guess: you probably have a grandmother, like I have. She's blind, and for my entire life she hasn't let me go anywhere, so that I've practically forgotten how to talk at all. And when I was misbehaving myself a couple of years ago, she saw there was no holding me, so she called me to her and pinned my dress to hers. And so we sit for days on end together: she knits stockings, blind as she is; I sit next to her sewing or reading aloud to her. It's a strange way of going on but I've been fastened to her for two years now—'

'Oh, good heavens, that's awful! Oh no, indeed, I have no grandmother like that.'

'Well if not, how is it you can just sit at home? . . .'

'Listen, do you want to know the sort of person I am?'

'Yes, yes, I do!'

'In the strict sense of the word?'

'In the strictest sense of the word!'

'If you must know, I'm a character.'

'A character? What sort of a character?' the girl cried, breaking into laughter as if she hadn't done the like for a year. 'You really are a joy to be with! Look: here's a bench; let's sit down. Nobody comes by here, nobody will overhear us and—well, do start your story! Because you can't talk me out of it; you do have a story to tell and you're just trying to keep it dark. In the first place, what do you mean by character?'

'Character? A character is an eccentric, a ridiculous individual!' I replied, lauhing heartily in the wake of her childlike hilarity. 'That's what a character is. Listen: do you know what a dreamer is?'

'A dreamer! Well, of course I do! I'm a dreamer myself. Sometimes, when I'm sitting next to granny, all sorts of things cross my mind. Once you start daydreaming, you get so carried away—I might easily be marrying a Chinese prince ... But sometimes it can be a good thing—to dream. Still, who knows if it is really—especially if you have other things on your mind as well', added the girl, this time rather gravely.

'Splendid! Seeing as you've married a Chinese prince, it follows that you will understand me completely. So, listen to me ... But forgive me: I still don't know your name.'

'At long last! You took your time about that, didn't you?'

'Oh lord, it never even entered my head, I was enjoying myself so...'

'My name is Nastenka.'

'Nastenka! And is that all?'

'All? Isn't it enough, you insatiable man!'

'Enough? It's a great deal, on the contrary, a very great deal, Nastenka, kind-hearted girl that you are to let me call you Nastenka straight away!'

'I should just think so! Well?'

'Well then, Nastenka, just listen to this ridiculous tale.'

I seated myself next to her, struck a pompously pedantic attitude, and began as if I were reading aloud:

'In Petersburg, Nastenka, if you aren't already aware of it, there are some moderately strange nooks and crannies. Such places seem not to be visited by the sun that shines for all the folk of Petersburg, but by another sun altogether, specially created for such corners, a sun that shines with a quite different, peculiar light. In these corners, sweet Nastenka, a totally different sort of life exists, quite unlike that which flourishes around us here; the kind that might exist in some never-never land, not here in the oh-so-serious age we live in. That other life is a mixture of the purely fantastic, the fervently idealistic, and at the same time (alas, Nastenka!) the dully prosaic and commonplace, if not the incredibly banal.'

'Heavens above! What a preamble! What on earth are you leading up to?'

'You shall hear, Nastenka (I believe I shall never tire of calling you Nastenka), you shall hear that strange people dwell in these corners—dreamers. The dreamer—if a precise definition is required—is not a person, but a sort of genderless creature. He usually prefers to settle in some inaccessible spot, as if to hide from the very daylight, and once he has taken up residence, he grows attached to it like a snail, or at least like that amusing creature which is both animal and house, and is called a tortoise. Why do you think he is so enamoured of his four walls, inevitably painted green, smoke-begrimed, dismal, and unpardonably fouled by tobacco? Why does this ridiculous individual, when one of his few acquaintances comes to see him (the upshot being that all such acquaintances make themselves scarce), greet him in such an embarrassed fashion, adopt a totally different expression—so flustered that he might have committed some crime within his four walls, taken up counterfeiting banknotes or scribbling verses to a magazine, with an anonymous letter announcing that the real poet has died, and that his friend regards it as his sacred duty to publish his effusions? Tell me, Nastenka, why is it that conversation cannot get started between the two of them? Why is there no laughter, no spirited repartee darting from the tongue of this casual visitor and his perplexed friend, who on other occasions enjoys both repartee and a good laugh, as well as talk of the fair sex and other light-hearted topics? And why is it, for goodness' sake, that this friend, no doubt a recent acquaintance on his first visit—because, things being what they are, there won't be a second—why is this friend in turn so embarrassed, so awkward, for all his wit (assuming he has any), as he gazes at the averted face of the host? The latter, for his part, is now completely at a loss, fairly at his wits' end after titanically vain efforts to ease things along and brighten up the conversation, to show that he too is capable of being worldly, talking of the fair sex and hoping through this effort at ingratiation to make a good impression on the poor man who has so grievously erred in paying him a visit. Why, for heaven's sake, does the visitor make a sudden grab for his hat and hastily take his leave, suddenly recalling some business of unprecedented urgency, somehow extricating his hand from the hot pressure of his host, who is trying all he knows to demonstrate his remorse, and salvage what has gone amiss? Why does the departing friend chuckle as he goes out of the door, vowing to himself on the spot never to come and see this odd fish again, even though the odd fish is at bottom the most capital of fellows? And yet at the same time he is unable to deny his fancy a little indulgence, namely to compare, however remotely, the countenance of his recent host during the entire time of their encounter to the look of a wretched kitten, rumpled, terrified, and generally ill-treated to the point of utter bewilderment by the children who have treacherously ensnared it, and which has eventually taken refuge in the darkness under a chair? There for a whole hour at leisure it must bristle and snort its fill and wash its aggrieved little muzzle with both paws and for long afterwards take a jaundiced view of nature and life—even the scraps from the master's dinner, saved for it by a compassionate housekeeper.'

'Look here', interrupted Nastenka, who had been absorbing all this in wide-eyed and open-mouthed astonishment. 'Now listen: I am absolutely in the dark as to why all that took place and why exactly you're putting such absurd questions; but what I do know for certain is that all these incidents happened to you without a shadow of doubt, word for word.'

'Absolutely true', I replied with the gravest of expressions.

'Well, if it's absolutely true, go on with the story', responded Nastenka, 'because I would very much like to know how all this is going to end.'

'You want to know, Nastenka, what our hero did in his corner, or rather—I, because the hero of this whole business is me—my very own humble self; you want to know why I was agitated and thrown off balance all day after the sudden visit of a friend? You want to know why I was in a fluttter, blushing when my room door was opened, why I couldn't cope with my visitor and broke down so shamefully under the weight of my own hospitality?'

'Yes, yes I do', Nastenka replied. 'That's the whole point. But one thing: you tell the story beautifully, but couldn't you make it just a little less so? It's as if you were reading from a book.'

'Nastenka!' I said in a tone of stern solemnity, trying hard not to laugh. 'Sweet Nastenka, I know I tell the tale beautifully, but I'm sorry, I can't tell it any other way. At this moment, sweet Nastenka, at this moment, I am like that spirit of King Solomon's,* who was in an earthenware jar for a thousand years, under seven seals, and who at length had those seals removed. Sweet Nastenka, now that we have come together again after such a lengthy separation—because I have known you for ever so long, Nastenka, I have been searching for someone for ever so long, and this is a sign that it was you I was seeking and it was fated that we should meet—at this moment, a thousand valves have opened within my brain, and I must pour forth a river of words or I shall suffocate. And so, I beg you not to interrupt me, Nastenka, just listen, meekly and obediently; otherwise I won't go on.'

'Oh, no—no—no, God forbid! Go on! I shan't say a word from now on.'

'Very well: there is in my day, dear Nastenka, one hour which I cherish above all others. It is precisely that hour when all business, duties, and engagements cease, and everyone hurries off home to have dinner, or a lie down, and while on the way entertains other cheerful notions touching the evening, the night, and the rest of the free time he has at his disposal. At this time of day, our hero too—allow me, Nastenka, to tell this in the third person, because it would be horribly embarrassing to do so in the first—so then, our hero too, who has not been without occupation, goes striding along after the others at this hour. But an odd hint of pleasure flits across his pale, almost haggard face. He gazes, a prey to emotion, at the evening sunset, slowly fading in the cold Petersburg sky. I say gazes, but that's not true: rather, he contemplates in a detached fashion, as if weary or simultaneously preoccupied with some other, more engrossing matter, and so only able to spare fleeting, almost involuntary attention to his surroundings. He is pleased because, until the morrow, he has done with the *business* he finds so irksome, happy as a schoolboy released from the classroom back to his favourite games and pranks. Take a sideways look at him Nastenka: you'll see at once that this glad feeling has already soothed his feeble nerves and morbidly irritable imagination. Now he's deep in thought . . . About his dinner you think? The evening ahead? What his eye has lighted upon? Yonder gentleman of respectable appearance who has just bowed so elaborately to the lady riding past in that glittering carriage drawn by swift-footed steeds? No, Nastenka, what are such trifles to him now? By now he is revelling in the richness of *his own inner life*; somehow he has acquired sudden wealth, and it is fitting that the valedictory ray of the dying sun should sparkle so blithely before him and evoke from his kindled heart a veritable swarm of answering sensations. Now he barely notices the road where previously the most trivial incident would strike him. Now "The Goddess of Imagination"* (if you've read your Zhukovsky, dear Nastenka) has woven her golden warp with capricious hand, unfolding before him patterns of fantastic chimerical life—who knows, perhaps translated him with that capricious hand from the excellent granite pavement, along which he was making his way homeward, to the seventh crystalline heaven. Try stopping him now and asking him suddenly where he is standing, what streets he has traversed. He would most likely remember nothing about where he has been or where he is standing now; red with annoyance, he would be sure to come out with some lie just to save his face. That's why he started so, almost crying out as he cast about him in alarm, when a most respectable old lady, having lost her way, politely stopped him in the middle of the pavement and began asking him for directions.

'Scowling with vexation, he strides onward, scarcely aware that several passers-by have smiled at the sight of him and followed him with their eyes, or that a little girl, timorously making way for him, laughed out loud as she stared, all eyes, at his broad preoccupied smile and gesticulating arms. But that same power of imagination has caught up the old woman too in its frolicsome flight, along with the curious passers-by, the laughing girl; and the men who spend the night on their barges at this spot, blocking the Fontanka (supposing our hero to be walking along it); everything and everyone has been impishly woven into its design like flies in a spider's web, and with this new acquisition of his the eccentric has now entered his comforting den, sat down to dinner, dined, and come down to earth only when his servant, the melancholy and ever-doleful Matryona, has cleared the table and fetched him his pipe; come down to earth and recalled with astonishment that he has had his dinner while remaining totally oblivious as to how that had come about. It has got darker in the room; his heart is sad and forlorn; his entire realm of reverie has collapsed about him, crumbled away without trace, noiselessly and without fuss, passed away like a dream, and even he cannot call back the vision to his mind. But there is a vague kind of sensation which promps a faint, aching perturbation in his breast, a novel sort of tantalizing desire which tickles and excites his imagination, conjuring up unnoticed a whole host of new phantoms. Silence reigns in the little room; solitude and idleness nurture the fancy; it flares up a little, seething gently like the water in old Matryona's coffee-pot, as she placidly busies herself nearby in the kitchen brewing up her cook's coffee. Now here it comes, starting to break through in flashes; the book, taken up pointlessly, at random, falls from my dreamer's hand before he reaches the third page. His imagination is roused up and attuned once more, then, all of a sudden, a new enchanting world, with all its glittering vistas, once more shines before him. A new dream, new happiness! A new draught of subtle, sensual poison! Ah, what did our real life hold for him? In his corrupted view, our lives, yours and mine, Nastenka, are so slow, so indolent, so sluggish; in his view we are all discontented with our lot, wearied-out by our lives! And actually it really is true; see how at first sight we treat each other so coldly and sullenly, almost angrily. "Poor things!" thinks my dreamer. And no wonder! Just look at these magical figments, taking shape before him, so fascinatingly intricate, stretching out before him, so boundlessly wide, an entrancing, animated spectacle, where the hero in the foreground is of course our dreamer in propria persona. See the variety of incident, the endless stream of rapturous visions. Perhaps you ask what he is dreaming about? Why ask? He dreams about everything . . . the role of the poet, at first unacknowledged, afterwards crowned with bays; friendship with Hoffman; Saint Bartholomew's night; Diana Vernon; Ivan the Terrible's heroic part in the taking of Kazan; Clara Mowbray; Effie Deans; Huss before the council of prelates; the rising of the dead men in *Robert the Devil* (remember the music? It smells of the cemetery!); about Minna and Brenda; the battle on the Berezina; the reading of an epic at the home of the Countess V—— D——; Danton; Cleopatra *e I suoi amanti*; the little house in Kolomna;* and about his own little burrow, and the dear creature who listens to him on a winter's evening, wide-eyed and open-mouthed, as you are listening to me at this moment, my little angel . . . No, Nastenka, what is there, what can there be for an indolent sensualist like him in the sort of life that you and I so long for? It is an impoverished, pitiable existence, so he thinks, failing to foresee that for him too, perhaps, the dismal hour will strike when he would exchange all his fantasy-ridden years for one day of this pitiable life—and do it without expectation of any joy or happiness; nor in that hour of sadness, remorse, and boundless grief, will he be concerned to choose. But until it arrives, that grim time, he desires nothing, because he is above desire, he has everything because he is surfeited, because he is the artist of his own life and creates it for himself by the hour as the mood takes him. And how easily, how naturally this fabulous fantasy-world is brought into being! As if it were not a figment at all! If truth be told, at times he is ready to believe that this life is not a product of emotional excitement at all, no mirage, no delusion of the imagination, but the true reality, the genuine article, the actual! Tell me why, Nastenka, pray tell me, why breathing becomes so difficult at such moments? Why does some magical or mysterious force quicken the dreamer's pulse, force tears to his eyes, and flame to his pale, damp cheeks, his every fibre suffused with an irresistible joy? Tell me why entire sleepless nights flash by in an inexhaustible blithe happiness, and when the dawn shines in through the windows, pink and radiant, and daybreak illumines the cheerless room with that uncertain fantastical light we know in Petersburg, does our dreamer, worn out and weary, throw himself on to his bed and fall asleep amid the blissful afterglow of his painfully shaken spirit and with such a languishingly sweet pain about his heart?

'Yes, Nastenka, he surrenders to the illusion and cannot but believe that a real and genuine passion is agitating his soul, that there is something vital and tangible in his disembodied visions! And what an illusion it is—take for example the love which has entered his breast with all its inexhaustible joy, all its wearying torments ... One glance at him will convince you! Would you believe it to look at him, sweet Nastenka, that he has never actually met the woman he has loved so much in his ecstatic daydreaming? Can it really be that he has only seen her in seductive visions and was this passion but a dream? Have they not really and truly passed* so many years of their lives hand in hand —the two of them alone, the world well lost, linking their own world, their own life each to each? Can it be that she, late in the day, when the hour of parting was at hand, did not lie miserably weeping on his breast, oblivious of the storm breaking beneath the grim heavens, deaf to the winds that snatched and bore away the teardrops from her dark lashes? Surely all that was no dream—and the garden, bleak, desolate, and wild, with its moss-grown paths, sequestered, mournful, where they had walked so often together, "so long and tenderly"! And this strange ancestral house in which she lived for so long, alone and sad with her morose old husband, forever taciturn and peevish, frightening them, as, childlike and timorous, they concealed their love from one another in joyless apprehension? The agonies they endured, the terror they felt in the chaste innocence of their affection, and (naturally, dear Nastenka) the malice they endured from other people. Ye gods, did he really not encounter her subsequently, far from their native shores, under the hot noonday of an alien southern sky, in the wondrous eternal city, at a glittering ball, to the thunderous sound of music, in a palazzo (certainly a palazzo), drowned in a sea of lights, on that balcony entwined with myrtle and roses, where she, recognizing him, removed her mask with such haste, and whispering "I am free" fell trembling into his arms, as with a cry of ecstasy they clung to each other, instantly forgetting their grief, their separation, and all the torments, the gloomy mansion and the old man, the cheerless garden in their distant homeland, and the bench where, after a final passionate kiss, she had torn herself from his arms, numb with tortured despair? . . .

'Ah, you must agree Nastenka, you too would start up and blush with embarrassment, like a schoolboy who has just stuffed into his pocket an apple stolen from a neighbour's garden, if a tall, strapping lad, a breezy clown of a friend dropping in unannounced, opened your door and shouted, all innocent: "I've just got here this minute from Pavlovsk, old man!" God in heaven! The old count has died, unspeakable happiness is at hand—and enter a person from Pavlovsk!'

I lapsed into an emotional silence, having concluded my emotional outpourings. I remember feeling a terrible urge to laugh out loud, whatever the consequences, because I already sensed a malevolent imp stirring within me, I had got a lump in my throat, my chin started trembling, and my eyes grew ever moister . . . I expected Nastenka, who had been listening to me with her intelligent eyes open wide, to burst out irrepressibly into her gay childlike laughter, and was regretting that I had gone so far; I shouldn't have told her of what had been so long raging within my heart I could recite it like a book. I had long since passed sentence on myself, and now couldn't help reading it out, to make a clean breast of things, though not with any expectation of being understood; but to my astonishment, she said nothing, and after a pause pressed my hand lightly and asked with a certain diffident concern:

'You don't mean that you have really lived all your life like that?'

'All my life, Nastenka', I replied. 'All my life, and it seems I will end it the same way!'

'No, you mustn't', she said, troubled. 'That will not happen; that way I might spend all my life with my grandmother. Look, you know living like that's not good for you?'

'I do, Nastenka, I do!' I exclaimed, giving vent to my emotions at last. 'And now I know more than ever that I have squandered all my best years! I realize that now, and the knowledge is the more painful because God has sent you to me, my good angel, to tell me and demonstrate the fact. Now, as I sit next to you and talk with you, I feel positively terrified of the future, because in that future loneliness lurks once more, again that musty, pointless existence; and what will there be for me to dream about, when close to you I have already been so happy in the real world. Ah, be gracious, dear girl that you are, for not turning me away at once, so that I can say I have lived at least two evenings in my life!'

'Oh, no, no!' cried Nastenka, tears starting to shine in her eyes. 'No, it won't be like that any more. We won't part this way! What are two evenings!'

'Ah, Nastenka, Nastenka! Do you realize how you have reconciled me to myself? Do you realize that I will no longer think so badly of myself as I have done at times? Do you realize that I will perhaps no longer agonize over having sinned and committed crimes during my life, because that sort of life is a sin and a crime in itself! And don't think I have exaggerated anything to you, please don't think that Nastenka, because sometimes such anguish overwhelms me, such anguish . . . because at moments like that I start to think that I am incapable of living a proper life, I seem already to have lost any sort of judgement, any apprehension of the real and actual; because after all, I have cursed my very self;

because after my nights of fantasy come moments of sobriety which are appalling! Meanwhile you hear the human crowd thundering and eddying around you in a living whirlwind, you hear and see people living—living in reality, you see that for them life is not something forbidden, their life does not fly asunder like dreams, like visions; it perpetually renews itself, is forever young, and no one hour is like any other; meanwhile how dreary and monotonously commonplace is this faint-hearted fantasy, the slave of a shadow, an idea, a slave of the first cloud that suddenly obscures the sun and afflicts with misery the heart of the true Petersburger who so cherishes his sun—and what fantasy can there possibly be in misery? You sense that it will at length grow weary, that it is exhausting itself in constant tension, this *inexhaustible* fantasy, because after all one matures, outgrows one's former ideals: they are shattered into dust and fragments; and if you have no other life, it behoves you to construct one from those same fragments.

'Meanwhile, the soul demands and seeks out something quite other! And the dreamer vainly rakes through his old longings like ashes, seeking in those ashes at least a few sparks that might be fanned into a fire to warm his chilled heart and resurrect anew in him that which was formerly so sweet, that which touched his soul, stirred his blood, tore the tears from his eyes, and so richly deceived him! Do you realize, Nastenka what things have come to? Do you know that I am compelled to celebrate the anniversary of my own sensations, the anniversary of what was formerly so precious to me, but never actually existed—because that anniversary is celebrated in memory of those same silly, disembodied dreamings—and do this because even those silly dreams are no more, since I lack the wherewithal to earn them: even dreams have to be earned, haven't they? Do you realize that on certain dates I enjoy recalling and visiting those places where I was once happy after my own fashion? I enjoy constructing my present in accord with things now irrevocably past and gone, and I often drift like a shadow, morose and sad, without need or purpose, through the streets and alleyways of Petersburg. What memories there are! I recall, for instance, that it was exactly one year ago, here at this precise time, that I wandered along the same pavement as lonely and depressed as I am now. I remember that even then my dreams were sad, and although things were no better back then, there's still the feeling that living was somehow easier and more restful, that there wasn't this black thought which clings to me now; there were none of these pangs of conscience, bleak, and gloom-laden which give me no peace by day or night. You ask yourself: where are your dreams now? And you shake your head and say how swiftly the years fly by! And you ask yourself again: what have you done with your best years, then? Where have you buried the best days of your life? Have you lived or not? Look, you tell yourself, look how cold the world is becoming. The years will pass and after them will come grim loneliness, and old age, quaking on its stick, and after them misery and despair. Your fantasy world will grow pale, your dreams will fade and die, falling away like the yellow leaves from the trees . . . Ah, Nastenka! Will it not be miserable to be left alone, utterly alone, and have nothing even to regret—nothing, not a single thing . . . because everything I have lost was nothing, stupid, a round zero, all dreaming and no more!'

'Come, don't make me feel any more sorry for you!' said Nastenka, wiping away a teardrop which had rolled from her eye. 'That's all done with! Now we will be together; now, whatever happens to me, we shall never part. Listen to me. I'm a simple girl, with not much schooling, although my grandmother did hire a tutor for me; but I really do understand you because everything that you have recounted to me just now I lived through myself when granny fastened me to her dress. Of course, I couldn't have told it as well as you, I've not had much schooling', she added shyly, still feeling a certain respect for my pathetic discourse and high-flown style. 'But I'm very glad that you have been completely frank with me. Now I do know you properly, through and through. And do you know what? I want to tell you my story too, all of it, keeping nothing back, and afterwards you will give me your advice. You're a very intelligent man; do you promise to advise me?'

'Ah, Nastenka', I responded, 'although I've never acted as an adviser before, let alone an intelligent one, I can see now that if we are to live like this always, that would be a most intelligent thing to do, and we will give one another lots and lots of intelligent advice! Now, my pretty Nastenka, what advice do you need then? Tell me straight out; I'm in such a good mood, happy, brave, and clever, I'll have lots to say.'

'No, no!' Nastenka interposed, laughing. 'It's not one bit of sound advice I need. What I need is warm, human advice as if you had loved me all your life!'

'Agreed, Nastenka, agreed!' I exclaimed rapturously. 'And if I had loved you for twenty years, I couldn't love you more than I do now!'

'Your hand!' said Nastenka.

'There it is', I responded, giving her my hand.

'So then, let us begin my story!'

Nastenka's Story

HALF the story you already know, that is, you know that I have an old grandmother . . .'

'If the second half is as brief as that . . .' I broke in, laughing.

'Be quiet and pay attention. Before I start, one condition; don't interrupt or I could easily lose track. So, do listen quietly.

'I have an old grandmother. I came to her when I was just a little girl, because my mother and father had both died. I presume she must have been better off at one time, because even now she keeps recalling better days. It was she who taught me French and afterwards hired a tutor. When I was 15 (I'm 17 now), our lessons came to an end. That was the time when I was naughty: what it was I did I shan't tell you: suffice it to say that it was only a minor misdemeanour. But grandma called me to her one morning and said that as she was blind, she wouldn't be able to keep an eye on me. Then she took a pin and fastened my dress to hers and there and then said that was how we should sit ever after, unless of course, I mended my ways. At all events, I simply couldn't

get away at first: working, reading or doing lessons, I was
always at her side. Once I attempted to trick her and talked
Fekla into taking my place. Fekla is our housemaid and she's
deaf. She sat down where I normally did, while grandma fell
asleep in her armchair and I set off to see a girlfriend not far
away. Well, it all ended in tears. Granny woke up in my
absence and asked some question, thinking I was still sitting
quietly in my place. Fekla could see she was asking something, but couldn't hear what it was, and after much cogitation
over what to do, unfastened the pin and took to her heels . . .'

At this point Nastenka broke off and started to rock with
laughter. I joined in, whereupon she stopped at once.

'Look, you mustn't make mock of granny. I'm laughing
because it's ridiculous . . . what on earth can I do if granny
really is like that? I still love her a little bit. Well, I really got
into trouble that time: I was sat down next to her at once and
God forbid I should budge an inch.

'So then, I forgot to tell you that we have, that is my
grandmother has, a house of her own, just a little one, only
three windows; it's all made of wood and as old as granny is;
there's an attic upstairs. Well, one day a new lodger moved
in . . .'

'So there must have been an old lodger?' I remarked in
passing.

'Yes, of course there was', responded Nastenka. 'And he
could keep quiet better than you. Actually, he could hardly
move his tongue. He was a wizened old fellow, dumb, blind,
and lame, so that eventually he couldn't go on living in this
world, and he died; then we had to get a new lodger, because
otherwise we couldn't get by: that and grandmother's pension
is virtually all the income we have. As luck would have it, the
new lodger was a young man, a stranger, not a local man.
Since he didn't haggle over terms, grandmother accepted
him, then asked: "Well, Nastenka, is our lodger young or
what?" I had no intention of lying: "He's not exactly young,
grandmother, but, you know, not an old man." "Well, is he
good-looking?" enquired grandmother.

'Again I didn't want to tell a lie. "Yes, he is, grandmother!"
But granny said: "Dear me, that's a nuisance, that's a

nuisance! Now I'm telling you granddaughter, don't go getting carried away. What is the world coming to! Just a paltry lodger, shouldn't wonder, but good-looking too: wasn't like that in the old days!"

'It was always the old days with granny. She was younger back then. And the sun was warmer, cream stayed fresher longer—everything was wonderful then. So there I sat quietly thinking to myself: why on earth was grandma giving me ideas, asking whether the lodger was young and handsome? But that was all, just a thought, then I started counting stitches again, knitting a stocking, and forgot all about it.

'So, one morning the lodger came in to remind us that we had promised to wallpaper his room. Granny is fond of her own voice and took her time about getting round to: "Go to my bedroom, Nastenka, and fetch my abacus." I jumped up at once, going quite red for some reason, and quite forgetting that I was still pinned to her; I didn't think to unfasten myself quietly so that the lodger wouldn't see—I tore myself away, disturbing granny's chair. When I saw that the lodger now knew all about me, I blushed and stood there transfixed before bursting into tears—so painfully ashamed I could have died. Granny shouted: "Well, what are you standing there for?" which made me feel still worse ... When the lodger saw that I was embarrassed at his being there, he excused himself and went away at once.

'After that, I died at every noise out in the passage. There, I thought, that would be the lodger coming; and just in case I would quietly unfasten the pin. But it never was him. He never came. A fortnight went by; the lodger sent word through Fekla that he had a lot of good French books, so I could read them if I wished; and might not grandmother like me to read them to her and keep her amused? Granny gratefully fell in with this, though she kept asking whether they were suitably moral ones because if they were immoral, then you can't possibly read them Nastenka, she said, you'll learn wicked things.

'"What will I learn, granny? What do they have in them?"

'"Oh", she said, "they describe how young men lead decent

girls astray; how they pretend they want to marry them and carry them off from their parents' house, then cast these wretched girls to the mercy of the fates and they perish in the most lamentable fashion. I've read lots of books like that", said granny, "and it's all so beautifully described that you could sit up all night reading them on the sly. So", says she, "just see you don't read them Nastenka. What sort of books has he sent then?"

'"They're all Walter Scott novels, granny."

'"Walter Scott novels! You mean he's not been up to anything? Have a good look now, make sure he hasn't slipped some love-note in there."

'"No", I said. "There's no note, granny."

'"Now you just look inside the binding; they sometimes tuck them inside the binding, the rascals!"

'"No, granny, there's nothing inside the bindings either."

'"Well, I should think not indeed!"

'So we started reading Walter Scott and got through nearly half of them in a month or so. After that he kept sending more and more, including Pushkin, so that eventually I doted on my books and stopped dreaming about marrying a Chinese prince.

'That was how matters stood when I chanced to run into our lodger on the stairs. Granny had sent me to fetch something. He came to a halt; I blushed and so did he; then he laughed and said hello and asked after granny's health. "Well, have you read the books?" he enquired. I replied: "Yes." "Which one did you like best, then?" So I said: "I enjoyed *Ivanhoe* and Pushkin the best of all." That was all on that occasion.

'A week later I bumped into him again on the staircase. This time, granny had not sent me; I had gone of my own accord for some reason. It was after two and the lodger was just coming home. "Hello", said he. "Hello", I replied.

'"Don't you find it dull sitting all day next to your grandmother?"

'I don't know why, but as soon as he asked me that, I grew flustered and went red; once more I felt annoyed, doubtless because others had started plying me with questions about that as well. I made to go off without answering, but the effort was too great.

'"Listen", he said. "You're a nice girl. I apologize for talking to you like this but I assure you I have more concern for you than your grandmother has. Have you no girlfriends at all you can go out and visit?"

'I told him I hadn't. There had been Mashenka, but she had gone away to Pskov.

'"Look", said he, 'would you like to go to the theatre with me?"

'"The theatre? But what about granny?"

'"Well, you just quietly . . ."

'"No", I said, "I wouldn't want to deceive her. Goodbye, sir!"

'"Well, goodbye then", he said. Nothing more was said.

'But after dinner he came to us; he sat down and talked with granny for a long time, enquiring whether she ever went out anywhere, of whether she had any friends—then he suddenly brought out: "I took a box at the opera today: they're doing *The Barber of Seville*; some friends were going but they cried off and I'm left with a spare ticket."

'"*The Barber of Seville*!" cried granny. "Was that the barber they used to do in the old days?"

'"Yes", said he. "It's the self-same barber", this said with a glance at me. I had realized his intentions and flushed as my heart leapt with anticipation!

'"Well of course", said granny, 'of course I know it! In the old days I played Rosina myself in our home theatricals!"

'"Would you like to come today then?" said the lodger. "My ticket will go to waste if not."

'"Yes, we could well go", said granny. 'Why not, after all? My Nastenka here has never been to the theatre."

'Heavens, how marvellous! We at once sorted out everything we needed, got ourselves ready, and set off. Granny might be blind but she did feel like listening to the music, and besides, she is a kind-hearted old thing: she really did it for my sake, we'd never have made the effort on our own. I can't begin to tell you the effect *The Barber of Seville* had on me, but all that evening our lodger kept giving me such sweet looks and talked so agreeably, that I realized at once he meant to try me out next day and see if I would go with him alone. Well, how wonderful! I went to bed so proud and elated, and my heart beat so that I felt a little feverish and dreamed all night of *The Barber of Seville*.

'I imagined that after that he would drop in more and more often—but not a bit of it. His visits ceased almost entirely. He would call in something like once a month, and then only to invite us to the theatre. We went with him once or twice, but I wasn't at all happy about that. I could see that he was just sorry for me because I was so much under granny's thumb, and there was no more to it than that. As time went on something came over me: I couldn't sit still, I couldn't read or work at anything; sometimes I would laugh and do something to spite granny. At other times I just cried. Eventually I lost weight and was on the verge of becoming really ill. The opera season ended and our lodger stopped coming altogether; whenever we met—always on that same staircase of course—he would bow silently, so gravely it seemed he had no wish to say anything, and be out on the porch while I was still standing half-way up the stairs, red as a beetroot, because the blood rushed to my head whenever I encountered him.

'The end came. Exactly a year ago in May, the lodger came to tell my grandmother that he had finished his business here and had to go off to Moscow again for a year. As soon as I heard that, I went ashen and dropped on to my chair like a dead thing. Grandma noticed nothing, while he, after announcing that he was leaving us, said his goodbyes and left the room.

'What was I to do? I thought and thought in mounting despair until I finally made up my mind. He was due to leave the next day and I resolved to bring matters to a head when granny had gone to bed. And so I did. I made all my dresses up into a bundle, all the underthings I needed, then, with bundle in hand and feeling more dead than alive, I made my way up to our lodger in the attic. It seemed to take me all of an hour to climb those stairs. When I opened his door, he cried out on seeing me. He thought I was a ghost and rushed to get me a drink of water, because I could barely stand up. My heart was beating so fast that my head ached, and I couldn't think clearly. When I did finally recover myself, I began by placing my bundle squarely on his bed, seated myself next to it, covered my face, and wept floods of tears. He seemed to understand everything in a flash and stood pale before me, his gaze so sad my heart fairly broke.

' "Look", he began. 'Look, Nastenka, there's nothing I can do; I'm a poor man; at the moment I have nothing, not even a decent job; how on earth would we live if I married you?"

'We talked for a long time, but eventually I worked up to a frenzy and said that I couldn't live with granny, that I would run away, I didn't want to be fastened to her, and that I could go to Moscow if he wanted me to, because I couldn't live without him. Everything within me spoke at once—shame, pride, and love. I almost fell on to the bed in convulsions. I was so terrified of a refusal!

'He sat for some minutes in silence, then got up, came over to me and took my hand.

' "Listen my good, sweet Nastenka", he began, as tearful as I was. "Listen to me. I swear to you that if ever I am able to marry, you will certainly be the one to complete my happiness. Look: I'm going to Moscow and I'll be there exactly a year. I am hoping to put my affairs in order. When I come back, and if you still love me, I vow to you that we shall be happy. At the moment, it's just impossible, I simply can't—I haven't the right to make any sort of promise. Still, I repeat, it will certainly happen if not in a year, then sometime; naturally, that depends on your not preferring someone else to me, because I cannot presume to bind you with any form of words."

'That was what he said to me, and he left the next day. We had both agreed that no word was to be said to granny. That was his wish. So, then, my story's nearly all done. Exactly one year has passed. He's come back, he's been here three whole days and . . . and . . .'

'And what?' I cried, eager to hear the outcome.

'He hasn't been to see me!' Nastenka replied, seeming to brace herself. 'Not a sign of him . . .

Here she stopped and, after a pause, dropped her head, covered her face with her hands, and began weeping in a way that wrung my heart.

I was utterly taken aback by the upshot of all this.

'Nastenka!' I began, in a diffident, ingratiating tone. 'Nastenka, for heaven's sake, don't cry! How do you know? Perhaps he isn't here yet . . .'

'He is! He is!' Nastenka returned. 'He's here, I know that. We arranged things back then, that evening before he went away: after we had said all that I have just now told you, and after making the arrangements, we came out here for a walk, along this same embankment. It was ten o' clock: we sat on this bench; I wasn't crying any more, it was lovely listening to him . . . He said, that as soon as he returned, he would come and see us, and if I didn't reject him, we would tell granny everything. Now he's come back, I know, and he hasn't been, he hasn't!'

And she broke down in tears once more.

'Good God, is there no way I can help in your misery?' I cried, leaping up from the bench in utter despair. 'Look, Nastenka, couldn't I at least go and see him? . . .'

'How could you possibly do that?' said she, raising her head suddenly.

'No, no, of course not!' I said, recollecting myself. 'I know: write him a letter.'

'No, that's impossible, I couldn't do that!' she replied firmly, but she had lowered her head and her eyes were averted.

'How can't you do it? Why on earth is it impossible?' I persisted, seizing on this idea. 'You know the sort of letter I mean, Nastenka! There are letters and letters and . . . Oh, Nastenka, it's true! Trust me, just trust me! You can rely on my advice. It can all be arranged. You took the initiative yourself—why do you now . . .'

'I can't, I can't! It would look as if I were pestering him . . .'

'Oh, dear little Nastenka that you are', I interrupted,

unable to suppress a smile. 'No, of course you're not; you are within your rights, since he made you a promise. Besides, I get the general impression that he is a man of tact, who conducted himself well', I pursued, with mounting elation at the logic of my own arguments and convictions. 'How did he act? He bound himself with a promise. He said he wouldn't marry anybody but you, if he married at all; he left you complete freedom to reject him even now . . . That being the case, you can make the first move, you have the right, you have the advantage over him, if only because, if you wanted to release him from his word . . .'

'Listen, how would you write?'

'Write what?'

'This letter of course.'

'I would start like this: "Dear Sir . . ."'

'Does it have to be "Dear Sir . . ."'

'Most certainly! Still, why should it? I think . . .'

'All right! Go on, go on!'

'"Dear Sir! Forgive me for . . ." No, come to think of it, no apologies necessary! The bare fact justifies everything in this case, just write:

'"Forgive my impatience in writing to you, but for a whole year, my happiness has been borne up by hope. Am I at fault in being unable to bear even one day of uncertainty? Now that you have come back, perhaps you have altered your intentions. In that case this letter will tell you that I do not complain or blame you. I do not blame you for the fact that I am powerless to guide your heart; such is my fate!

'"You are a gentleman. Do not smile or take offence at these eager lines of mine. Remember they are written by a poor girl, who is alone with no one to teach or advise her and that she has never been able to master her own heart. But do forgive me that even a moment's doubt should have stolen into my heart. You are incapable even in thought of hurting the one who loved you so and loves you still."'

'Yes, yes! That's exactly what I thought!' Nastenka cried, and gladness shone in her eyes. 'Oh, you have resolved my doubts, God must have sent you to me! Thank you. Oh, thank you!'

'For what? because God sent me?' I replied, gazing delight-edly at her radiant little face.

'That, for one thing.'

'Ah, Nastenka, we thank some people just for living alongside us. I thank you for the fact that you met me, and that I will remember you all my days!'

'Well all right, all right! And now, just listen carefully: we arranged back then that as soon as he returned, he would let me know by leaving me a letter in a certain place, with some friends of mine, decent, ordinary folk, who know nothing about all this; if he can't write me a letter, because you can't always say everything in a letter, then he would come here that very day at ten o'clock, where we arranged to meet. I already know he's arrived; but this is the third day and there has been no letter, nor any sign of him. I can't possibly get away from granny in the mornings. Tomorrow, please give my letter to those good people I told you of: they will forward it on and if there is an answer, bring it here in the evening at ten o'clock.'

'But the letter, the letter! The letter has to be written first! So all this can only be managed the day after tomorrow.'

'The letter . . .' replied Nastenka, slightly flustered. 'The letter . . . but . . .'

But she left the sentence unfinished. At first she averted her little face, blushed pink as a rose, and suddenly I felt a letter in my hand, evidently written long in advance, all ready and sealed. A familiar, sweet, graceful recollection stirred in my brain.

'R,o – Ro, s,i – si, n,a – na',* I began.

'Rosina!' we both began singing, I almost embracing her out of sheer delight, she blushing furiously as only she could, laughing through her tears, which trembled like pearls on her dark eyelashes.

'Dear me, that's enough, that's enough! Goodbye then!' she said hastily. 'There's the letter, there's the address to take it to. Goodbye, *au revoir*! Till tomorrow!'

She squeezed both my hands, bobbed her head, and flitted away along the lane like an arrow. I stood there for a long time following her with my eyes.

'Till tomorrow! Till tomorrow!' echoed in my brain as she disappeared from view.

THE THIRD NIGHT

TODAY has been dreary and rain-sodden, without a ray of hope, like my approaching old age. Such strange ideas oppress me, such dark sensations, such vague questions seething in my brain—and somehow I have neither strength nor desire to resolve them. It's beyond me to make sense of it all!

We shall not see each other today. When we parted last night the sky was starting to cloud over and a mist was rising. I told her that today would be nasty; she made no reply, she was disinclined to force herself to speak; for her this day was both bright and fine, without a single cloud to dim her felicity.

'If it rains, we shan't see each other!' she said. 'I shan't come.'

I had thought she would not even notice today's rain, but still she has not come.

Yesterday was our third rendezvous, our third white night . . .

Heavens, how joy and happiness lend beauty to a person! How the heart overflows with love! You seem to want to pour all it holds into the heart of another, so that everything turns to gaiety and laughter. And how infectious that gladness is! Yesterday the words held so much comfort, such kindliness towards me in her heart . . . how she danced attendance on me, so affectionate, how she cheered and soothed my heart! Ah, how flirtatious sheer happiness can be! And I took it all at face value; I thought she . . .

Good lord, though, how on earth could I have thought such a thing? How could I have been so blind, when it had all been appropriated by another, none of it was mine; when eventually even that same gentleness of hers, her solicitude, her love . . . yes, love for me—was nothing but gladness at the imminent prospect of a tryst with another, an urge to thrust her happiness on to me too? . . . When he failed to arrive, after we had waited in vain, she fell to frowning, she quailed and lost heart. Every movement, every word lost its former ease and playful high spirits. And, oddly enough, she redoubled her attentions towards me, as if sensing an instinctive urge to pour out on me what she sought for herself, and what she feared might not come about. My Nastenka was so timorous, so terrified that she seemed at last to realize that I was in love with her, and took pity on this wretched love of mine. So it is that when we are unhappy we sense more acutely the unhappiness of others; rather than dispersing, the emotion becomes focused . . .

I had come to her with a full heart and could barely wait for our meeting. I had no inkling of the feelings I have now, no thought that it might all go wrong. She was radiantly happy in her expectation of a reply. The reply was to be the man himself. He was supposed to come running at her call. She had arrived a whole hour before I did. At first she laughed loudly at everything, every word of mine amused her. I made as if to speak, then remained silent.

'Do you know why I am so happy, so happy to look at you? So fond of you today?'

'Well?' I asked, my heart trembling.

'The reason I like you is that you haven't fallen in love with me. You know, in your place, any one else might have started being a nuisance, badgering me with his sighing and moaning, but you're so sweet!'

At this, she gave my hand such a squeeze I almost cried out. She broke into a laugh.

'Goodness, such a friend!' she began a moment later, now quite grave. 'Really God must have sent you to me! I mean what would have become of me if you hadn't been with me? How unselfish you are! How fond you are of me! When I am married we'll be ever such good friends, more than brother and sister. I will love you almost as much as him . . .'

I suddenly felt an immense sadness at that moment; on the other hand, something like laughter began to stir in my heart.

'You're all on edge', said I. 'You're afraid; you're thinking he won't come.'

'Get away with you!' she rejoined. 'If I weren't so happy, I would most likely weep at your reproaches and lack of faith. Still, you've made me reflect and think deeply, but I'll leave that till later, and admit for now that you have spoken no more than the truth. Yes! I'm not myself somehow; I'm all anticipation and over-sensitive to everything. Still, that's enough about emotions! . . .'

Just at that moment there came the sound of footsteps and a passer-by loomed out of the darkness, walking towards us. We both started, and she barely kept from crying out. I dropped her hand and made as if to move off. But we were mistaken: it was not him.

'What are you afraid of? Why did you let go my hand?' she asked, proffering it once more. 'Well, why not? We'll meet him together. I want him to see our love for one another.'

'Our love for one another?' I cried.

'Ah, Nastenka, Nastenka!' I thought, 'How much you have said with that word. Love like that, Nastenka, can sometimes chill the heart and lie heavy on the soul. Your hand is cold, mine burns like fire. How blind you are, Nastenka! . . . Ah! How unbearable a happy person can be sometimes. But I cannot be angry with you! . . .'

At length my heart simply overflowed.

'Listen, Nastenka!' I cried. 'Do you know what has been the matter with me all day?'

'What then, what do you mean? Out with it now! What's been keeping you so quiet all this while?'

'Well firstly, Nastenka, when I had carried out all your commissions, handed over the letter, went to see your good people, afterwards . . . afterwards I came home and lay down.'

'Is that all, then?' she broke in, laughing.

'Yes, more or less', I returned, uneasily aware that my eyes were already filling with silly tears. 'I woke up an hour before we were due to meet, feeling that I hadn't slept at all. I don't know what was the matter with me. I was coming here intending to tell you all about it, as if time had stopped for me, as if the same emotion, the same feeling would stay with me for ever from that moment on, as if that one minute would stay with me for the whole of eternity, as if the whole of life had come to a halt for me ... When I awoke, I imagined that some long-familiar musical motif, heard somewhere, a forgotten delight, had now recurred to me. It seemed to have been demanding release from my soul for all my life and only now ...'

'Oh heavens above!' Nastenka broke in. 'What was all that supposed to mean? I can't understand a word you're saying.'

'Oh, Nastenka! I was trying to convey something of this weird feeling ...' I began in a plaintive tone, which still harboured a flicker of hope, utterly forlorn though it might be.

'Oh enough of that, stop it, do!' said she, seeing through it all instantly, the little minx!

All at once, she became unusually talkative, high-spirited, and flirtatious. She linked arms, laughing to make me laugh as well, and each embarrassed word of mine evoked such prolonged ringing laughter ... I began to lose all patience with her coquettish act.

'Look', she said. 'I really am a little annoyed that you haven't fallen in love with me. Make sense of the man after that! But still, Mister Unbending, you must give me credit for my straightforwardness. I keep telling you every passing silliness that comes into my head!

'Listen! Isn't that eleven o'clock?' I said, as a bell began its measured tolling from a distant city tower. She at once halted, ceased her laughing, and began to count.

'Yes, eleven', she said at length in a timid, irresolute voice.

I instantly repented of having frightened her by forcing her to count the chimes and cursed myself for my fit of spite. I felt miserable for her, without knowing how to redeem my transgression. I began reassuring her, deploying all manner of argument and evidence in devising excuses for his absence. Nobody could have been easier to deceive than she was at that moment; of course, anyone at such a juncture is glad to listen to any sort of reassurance, and doubly so if it contains even a hint of plausibility.

'Well, this is a ridiculous situation', I began, increasingly carried away, and marvelling at the extraordinary clarity of my arguments. 'He couldn't have come, anyway; you've hoodwinked me, Nastenka, and led me up the garden path so much I've even lost track of the time ... Just look at it this way: he can scarcely have got the letter yet; let's say he's prevented from coming, say he's writing a reply, the letter can't possibly get there earlier than tomorrow. I'll call for it at the crack of dawn and let you know straight away. A thousand and one things may have happened: he might have been out when the letter came and not even read it yet. It could be anything.'

'Yes, that's it!' responded Nastenka. 'I never thought of that; of course anything might have happened', she pursued, her voice all acquiescence, though there was another, more remote thought present, like an irritating dissonance. 'This is what you do', she went on. 'Tomorrow, go as soon as may be, and if you find anything let me know at once. You know where I live, don't you?' She began to repeat her address to me.

After that, she suddenly became so shyly affectionate towards me ... She seemed to listen closely to what I was saying to her, but when I asked her a question, she would make no reply, grow confused, and turn her little head away. I glanced at her eyes—I knew it, she was crying.

'Now then, what's this, what's this? Oh, what a baby you are! Behaving like a child! ... That's enough now!'

She tried to smile and recover herself, but her chin was quivering and her breast still heaved.

'I keep thinking of you', she said after a moment's pause. 'You are so kind, I would have to be made of stone not to feel that ... You know what crossed my mind just now? I was comparing you both. Why is he—not you? Why is he not like you? He's worse than you, even though I love him more than you.'

I made no reply. She seemed to expect me to say something.

'Of course it may be that I don't understand him properly as yet, haven't got to know him properly. You know, I seem always to have been afraid of him; he was always so grave, such a air of dignity. Of course I know that's just the outside; in his heart there's more affection than in mine ... I remember the way he looked at me that time, when I came to him with my bundle that time; but I still seem to feel too much respect for him; doesn't that show we're not equals?'

'No, Nastenka, no', I replied. 'It means that you love him more than anything in the world and a great deal more than yourself.'

'Yes, I suppose that's so', responded Nastenka naïvely, 'but, you know what crossed my mind just now? I won't talk about that now, though, just, you know, in general; it's been in my mind for a long time. Listen, why can't we all behave like brothers to one another? Why does even the best of men always keep something back, something unspoken from the other? Why not come straight out with what's in his mind, if it's something worth saying? As it is, everybody looks grimmer than he really is, as if everyone was afraid of bruisng their own feelings if they divulge them too soon . . .'

'Oh, Nastenka! That's the truth of it; it stems from a number of reasons, doesn't it?' I interrupted, keeping a tighter grip on my feelings at that moment than I had ever done.

'No, no!' she returned, deeply stirred. 'Take you, for instance, you're not like the others! I really don't know how to describe to you what my feelings are about this; but I think that you for instance . . . if only at this moment . . . I feel you are sacrificing something for my sake', she added shyly, with a swift glance at me. 'Do forgive me for talking to you like this: I'm only a simple girl, after all; I haven't seen much of the world yet, I mean, and really I can't put things properly sometimes', she added, her voice trembling for some concealed emotion, yet trying to smile at the same time. 'I just meant to tell you that I am grateful and that I feel all these things as well . . . Oh, may God grant you happiness for it! All that you were telling me about that dreamer of yours is completely untrue, or rather, I mean it doesn't apply to you. You're getting better, really you're quite a different person from the self you described. If you ever fall in love, may God give you happiness with her! I don't wish anything for her because I know she'll be happy with you. I know, I'm a woman myself, and you must believe what I tell you . . .'

She stopped talking and gave my hand a firm squeeze. Emotion prevented me from speaking either. Several minutes passed.

'Yes it's obvious he won't be coming today!' she said at length, lifting her head. 'It's too late! . . .'

'He'll come tomorrow', said I in my firmest and most reassuring voice.

'Yes', she broke in, brightening. 'I can see myself that he could only come tomorrow. So *au revoir*! Till tomorrow then! If it's raining I might not come. But I will the day after, come what may; be sure to be here; I want to see you and tell you all about it.'

As we were saying goodbye, she gave me her hand and said, gazing brightly at me:

'After all, we are together for always now, aren't we?'

Ah, Nastenka, Nastenka! If you only knew the loneliness I endure now!

When nine struck, I could not stay in my room; I got dressed and went out, the bad weather notwithstanding. I was there, sitting on our bench. I meant to go into their lane but fought shy of it and came back after a couple of steps, without a glance at their windows. I came back home in a depression such as I have never experienced. A dank and tedious time! If the weather had been fine I would have walked about there the whole night . . .

But till tomorrow, till tomorrow! Tomorrow she will tell me all about it.

There was no letter today, however. Still, that was bound to be the case. They are together by now.

THE FOURTH NIGHT

GOOD God! The way all this turned out! The upshot of it all!

I came at nine o'clock. She was already there. I saw her in the distance; she was standing as she had done then, the first time, leaning on the embankment railing, oblivious of my approach.

'Nastenka!' I called out, fighting to suppress my agitation.

She swiftly turned to me.

'Well?' she said. 'Well, quickly now!'

I looked at her in bewilderment.

'Where's the letter, then? You've brought the letter, haven't you?' she repeated, clutching at the rail.

'No, I haven't got any letter', I said at length. 'You mean he hasn't been here?'

She went horribly pale and stared at me for a long time without moving. I had shattered her final hope.

'Well, so be it!' she said finally, her voice breaking. 'Good luck to him, if he's leaving me in the lurch like this.'

She dropped her eyes, then made to look at me but couldn't. She fought down her agitation for another few minutes, then abruptly turned, leant on the balustrade, and dissolved into tears.

'There, there, that's enough now', I made to say, but as I looked at her, I hadn't the strength to go on—and what could I have said anyway?

'Don't try to console me', she said, as she wept. 'Don't say anything about him, don't tell me that he'll come and that he hasn't thrown me over in the cruel inhuman way he has. Why, for what reason? Surely there wasn't anything in my letter, that wretched letter? . . .

At this point, her voice was choked with sobs; it was heart-breaking to look at her.

'Ah, how inhumanly cruel it is!' she resumed. 'And not a line, not a line! He could have replied at least, that he did not need me, that he was rejecting me; but not a single line in three whole days! How easy he finds it to insult and hurt a poor, defenceless girl, whose only fault is that she loves him! What I've gone through these last three days! Good God, good God! When I remember how I went to him of my own accord that first time, how I abased myself, and wept, implored him for the merest drop of love . . . And after all that! . . . Listen', she said, turning to me, her small dark eyes a-glitter. 'It just can't be! It's impossible; it's not natural! Either you or I have been deceived; it could be that he didn't get the letter? Perhaps he knows nothing about it yet? How on earth can that be, judge for yourself and tell me, for heaven's sake, explain—because I can't understand it—how anyone can be as brutally cruel as he has been towards me! Not one word! The lowliest person in the world would be treated with more compassion. Perhaps he's heard something, perhaps someone has been telling him things about me?' she cried, addressing the question to me. 'What do you think? Tell me.'

'Listen Nastenka, I'll go and see him tomorrow on your behalf.

'Oh!'

'I'll ask him about the whole business, and tell him everything.'

'Oh, come now!'

'You'll have to write a letter. Don't say no, Nastenka, don't say no! I'll make him appreciate what you've done, he'll know all about it, and if . . .'

'No, my friend, no', she broke in. 'No more of that! Not a word, not one word from me, not a line—that's over and done with! I don't know him and I don't love him any more. I shall for—get him . . .'

She did not finish.

'Compose yourself, compose yourself, do! Sit down here, Nastenka', I said, seating her on the bench.

'I am perfectly composed. That's enough! It's all right! Just tears, they'll soon dry. Are you thinking I'll do away with myself, throw myself in the canal? . . .

My heart was full; I made to speak but could not do it.

'Listen!' she went on, taking my hand. 'Would you have acted like that? Would you have abandoned a girl who came to you of her own accord, would you have sneered openly and brazenly at her frail, silly heart? You'd have taken care of her? You'd have realized that she was all alone and unable to look out for herself, couldn't prevent herself from loving you, she was not to blame, that she wasn't to blame for goodness' sake ... she had done nothing! ... Oh, good grief, good grief ...'

'Nastenka! I cried out at length, unable to supress my agitation. 'Nastenka! You are tormenting me! You are wounding my heart, you're killing me, Nastenka! I can't keep silent! I have to speak out at last, and tell you wh..t has been raging here in my heart ...'

In saying this, I had half risen from the bench. She took my hand and stared at me in astonishment.

'What's the matter?' she said at length.

'Listen to me!' I said firmly. 'Listen to me, Nastenka! What I am about to tell you is just silliness, it can never be, just nonsense! I know nothing can come of it, but I simply cannot keep quiet any longer. In the name of that which is causing your present suffering, I plead forgiveness in advance! ...'

'What is it then? Well?' she said, no longer crying and staring fixedly at me, while a strange curiosity shone from her astonished eyes. 'What's the matter with you?'

'It can never be, but I love you, Nastenka! That's what! There, it's all out now!' I said, with a gesture. 'Now you will see whether you can talk to me as you have been just now, whether you can listen to what I have to tell you, for goodness' sake ...'

'Well what of it? What of it?' Nastenka interrupted. 'What about it, then? I've known for ages that you loved me, but I always thought it was just in a general sort of way ... Oh good heavens, good lord!'

'It was just like that at first, Nastenka, but now, now ... I'm in exactly the state you were in when you went to him with your bundle. Worse in fact, Nastenka, because then he didn't love anybody else, but you do ...'

'What is it you're trying to say? I really don't understand you at all. Look, what on earth are you telling me this for? No, I don't mean that, I mean why are you going on like this—and so sudden ... God! I'm talking nonsense! But you ...'

And Nastenka became totally confused. Her cheeks flamed; she dropped her eyes.

'What can I do, Nastenka, what on earth can I do? It's all my fault, I've abused your ... No, never, I'm not to blame, Nastenka: I sense it, feel it because my heart tells me I'm right, because I couldn't possibly hurt or offend you! I was your friend; well, I remain a friend; I haven't changed at all. Now it's my tears that are flowing, Nastenka. Let them flow, let them—they're not hurting anyone. They'll dry, Nastenka ...'

'Oh, sit down, do, sit down', said she, tugging me down on to the bench. 'Oh, good lord in heaven!'

'No, Nastenka! I won't sit down; I can't stay here any longer, you mustn't see me any more; I'll say what I have to say, then go. I just want to tell you, that you would never have realized I loved you. I would have preserved my secret. I wouldn't have tormented you at this moment with my selfishness. No! But just now I couldn't stand it any more; you brought it up yourself, it's your fault, it's all your fault, not mine. You can't drive me away from you ...'

'No, no, of course not, I'm not driving you away, no!' said Nastenka, concealing her embarrassment as best she could, poor thing.

'Not driving me away? And I was ready to run away myself. I will go, though, but first I'll tell you everything from the beginning, because when you were talking just now, I just couldn't sit still, when you were crying, when you were in agonies because of, well, because of (I have to say it, Nastenka) because you had been spurned, because your love had been rejected, I sensed, I felt so much love in my heart for you, Nastenka, so much love ... my heart just broke, and I ... I simply couldn't stay silent, I had to speak out, Nastenka, I had to speak!'

'Yes, yes! Speak to me, speak to me like that!' said Nastenka with an enigmatic gesture. 'You may think it odd my telling you like this, but ... go on! I'll explain afterwards! I'll explain everything!'

'You're taking pity on me, Nastenka; you're just sorry for me, my dear! What's done is done! What's said can't be unsaid! That's so, isn't it? Well then, now you know it all. Let that be the starting point. All right, then. Now everything's fine; listen though. When you were sitting there weeping, I was thinking to myself (ah, do let me tell you what I was thinking!), I thought (well of course I know it was impossible, Nastenka), I thought that you . . . I thought that somehow you . . . I mean, in some completely fortuitous fashion, might have ceased to love him. In which case—I was thinking this yesterday, and the day before that, Nastenka—in that case I would have made you fall in love with me, I most certainly would: you did say, didn't you, you said it yourself, that you had almost fallen in love with me in earnest. Well, what else? That's really about all I wanted to say; it just remains to tell you how it would have been if you had fallen in love with me, just that, nothing more! Listen to me, dear friend, because you are still my friend after all—of course, I am just an ordinary, impoverished individual, a nobody, but that's irrelevant (I'm straying from the point, but that's out of embarrassment, Nastenka), but I would have loved you, loved you so much that even if you had loved and gone on loving that unknown him, you would not have noticed my love as irksome in the slightest. All you would have sensed, all you would have felt every moment, would have been a grateful, grateful heart beating beside you, a burning heart which for you . . . Ah, Nastenka, Nastenka, what have you done to me! . . .'

'Oh, don't weep, I don't want you to cry', said Nastenka, rising swiftly from the bench. 'Let's go, get up and go together, don't cry though, don't cry', she kept saying, wiping away my tears with her handkerchief. 'Come, let's go now; I may have something to tell you . . . Yes, since he has abandoned and forgotten me now, although I still love him (I would not wish to delude you) . . . but listen, tell me. If, for example, I were to fall in love with you, I mean if I only . . . Ah, my friend, my friend! When I think, when I think of how I was hurting you when I laughed at your love, and praised you for not falling in love! . . . O God! How on earth didn't I foresee such a thing, how could I have been so stupid, but . . . well, all right, I've made up my mind, I'll tell you everything . . .'

'Listen, Nastenka, you know what? I'm going to leave you, so there! I'm just a torment to you. You've pangs of conscience because you laughed at me, but I don't want you, on top of your own grief . . . I certainly don't want that! Of course it's all my fault. Well, it's goodbye, Nastenka!'

'Stop a moment and listen to me: can you wait?'

'For what? What do you mean?'

'I love him; but that will pass, it's bound to, it can't help but pass; it's already passing, I can sense it . . . Who knows, it may be over this very day, because I detest him, because he was laughing at me, while you were weeping here with me, because you would not have spurned me like him, because you love me and he did not, because, last but not least, I love you myself . . . yes, love, love, the way you love me; I did say it first, you heard me didn't you? I love you because you are better than he is, because you're nobler, because he . . .'

The poor girl's agitation was too intense for her to finish. She placed her head on my shoulder, then on my chest, and gave way to bitter weeping. I tried to console her, talk her round, but she couldn't help herself; she kept squeezing my hand and saying between sobs: 'Wait a moment, wait a moment; I'll stop in a minute! I want to tell you . . . Don't imagine these tears—they're nothing, just a sign of weakness, just wait till they pass.' At length she stopped and wiped away the tears and we resumed our walk. I made to say something but she kept begging me to wait. We were both silent . . . Eventually she nerved herself and began to speak . . .

'This is the way of it', she began. Her voice was weak and quavering, but it held a ring that pierced me straight to the heart and ached there sweetly. 'You mustn't think I am so fickle and inconstant, that I find it easy to forget and betray . . . I loved him for a whole year and swear to God that I was never ever unfaithful to him, even in thought. He despised that; he laughed at me—so be it! But he has wounded me and insulted my feelings. I—I don't love him, because I can only love someone who is chivalrous and high-minded and understands me; because I am like that myself and he is unworthy of me—well, never mind. It's better this way than being deceived in my expectations later on and realizing the kind of man he was . . . Well, of course! Still who knows, my dear friend', she went on, pressing my hand, 'who knows, perhaps all this love of mine was a figment of my imagination, perhaps it all began as a trivial piece of mischief, because I was under granny's surveillance? Perhaps I ought to love another, not him, not a man like that, some other, who would have pity on me and, and . . . Well, enough of that', she broke off, panting with agitation. 'I only wanted to tell you that . . . I meant to say, that if, despite the fact that I love him (no, loved him), if despite that, you still say . . . if you feel that your love is so great that it can eventually displace the former love in my heart . . . if you wish to take pity upon me, and do not mean to abandon me to my fate, without hope or consolation, if you mean to love me for ever the way you do now, then I swear that my gratitude . . . that my love will eventually be worthy of your own . . . Will you take my hand now?'

'Nastenka!' I cried, choking with sobs. 'Nastenka! . . . Ah, Nastenka! . . .

'Well, that's enough, that's enough now. Quite enough!' she said, keeping her self-control with difficulty. 'Now everything's been said, hasn't it? Yes? And you're happy and I'm happy; not another word about it; wait a while; spare me . . . Talk about something else, for pity's sake! . . .

'Yes, Nastenka, I will! No more of this, now I'm happy, I . . . well, Nastenka, we'll talk about something else, quickly now, quickly; right! I'm ready . . .'

And neither of us knew what to say, we laughed, we cried, we spoke a thousand inane, incoherent words; we walked along the pavement, then suddenly came back and set off across the street; then came to a halt and re-crossed to the embankment; we were like children . . .

'I am living on my own at the moment', I said, 'but tomorrow . . . Well, of course, Nastenka, you know I'm a poor man, I only have twelve hundred, but that doesn't matter . . .'

'Of course not, and grandma has her pension; she won't be a burden. She has to be with us.'

'Of course she has . . . But there's Matryona . . .'

'Ah yes, and we've got Fekla as well.'

'Matryona's a good old soul. She's only got one drawback: she has no imagination, absolutely none at all; but that's all right! . . .

'It doesn't matter; they can live together; but you must move in with us tomorrow.'

'What do you mean? In with you? Very well, I'm ready . . .'

'Yes, you can be our lodger. We've got the attic upstairs; it's vacant. We did have a lady there, an old woman of noble family, but she's moved on and I know that granny wants to let the room to a young man; I said: "Why a young man?" And she said: "Well you know, I'm getting on, but don't go thinking I want to marry you off to him." I just knew that was what she had in mind . . .'

'Oh, Nastenka! . . .'

And we both laughed.

'That's enough now, that's enough. But where do you live? I've gone and forgotten.'

'Near ——sky Bridge. The Barannikov house.'

'That big building?'

'Yes, that's the one.'

'Oh yes, I know it, it's a fine place; still, you know, do be quick and move in with us . . .'

'Tomorrow it shall be, Nastenka, tomorrow; I owe a little there for the flat, but it's all right . . . I get my salary soon . . .'

'And you know what, I might start giving lessons; I'll study and then give lessons . . .'

'Well that's really marvellous . . . and I'll be getting a bonus soon, Nastenka . . .'

'So then, tomorrow you will be my lodger . . .'

'Yes and we'll go and see *The Barber of Seville*, because it's going to be on again soon.'

'Yes, we'll do that', said Nastenka, laughing. 'No, best if we see something other than *The Barber of Seville* . . .'

'Well, all right, something else; of course that would be better, I just wasn't thinking . . .'

So saying, we both walked along in a sort of daze, a fog, as if we didn't know ourselves what was happening to us. We would stop and talk for ages on one spot, then we would set off again lord knows where, more laughter, more tears . . .

Nastenka would suddenly want to go home and I didn't venture to prevent her, intending to see her all the way home; we would set off and inside a quarter of an hour find ourselves on the embankment, near our bench. Now she would heave a sigh and tears would start from her eyes again; I would lose heart, feel a chill . . . But she squeezed my hand at once and tugged me off again to walk and chatter and talk . . .

'Time I went home now; I think it's very late', said Nastenka at length. 'Enough of such childish behaviour!'

'Yes, Nastenka, though I'm sure I shan't be able to get to sleep; I shan't go home.'

'I don't think I'll get to sleep either, but see me to the house . . .'

'Of course I will!'

'But this time we'll go all the way to our apartment.'

'Of course we will, of course . . .'

'Word of honour? Because I do have to get back home sometime!'

'Word of honour', I replied, laughing . . .

'Let's go then!'

'Let's.

'Just look at that sky, Nastenka, just look! Tomorrow is going to be a wonderful day; the sky so blue, and what a moon! Look at that yellow cloud blotting it out, look, look! . . . No, it's slipped by. Look, look there! . . .'

But Nastenka was not looking at the cloud, she was standing mutely rooted to the spot; a moment later she started pressing timidly against me. Her hand began to tremble in mine; I glanced at her . . . she pressed harder against me.

At that moment, a young man walked past us. He came to an abrupt halt, gazed intently at us, then walked on a few paces. My heart quivered within me . . .

'Nastenka', I said in a low voice. 'Who is it, Nastenka?'

'It's him!' she whispered, pressing still closer and shaking against me . . . I could barely keep my feet.

'Nastenka! Nastenka! It's you!' came a voice from behind us, and at that moment, the young man came several steps nearer . . .

Lord, what a shriek she uttered! How she shuddered! She

tore herself from my arms and went fluttering to meet him!
... I stood and watched them, crushed. But she had scarcely
given him her hand, scarcely flung herself into his arms,
when she turned to me and was suddenly by my side, like
lightning, like the wind, and before I could recollect myself,
she put both arms round my neck and kissed me firmly and
ardently. Then without saying a word, she ran to him again,
took his arm, and tugged him along after her.

I stood there for a long time, looking after them ...
Eventually they disappeared from view.

MORNING

MY nights ended with the morning. It was a nasty day. Rain
was falling and beat dismally against my window panes; it was
dark in my little room and heavily overcast outside. My aching
head fairly swam; a fever was stealing through my limbs.

'A letter for you, master, by the town post, the postman
brought it', Matryona was pronouncing over me.

'A letter! Who from?' I shouted, leaping from my chair.

'That I don't know, master, have a look, maybe it says who
it's from.'

I broke the seal. It was from her!

'Ah forgive me, forgive me!' Nastenka had written. 'I beg
you on my knees to forgive me! I deluded both myself and
you. It was a dream, a phantom ... I have longed for you
today; forgive me, oh forgive me! ...

'Do not reproach me: I have not changed in the least
towards you; I said I would love you, and so I do, more than
love you. Oh God! If I could only love you both at once! Ah,
if only you were he!'

'Ah, if only he were you!' flashed through my brain. I
recalled your own words, Nastenka!

'God understands what I would do for you now! I know
you feel miserable and sad. I have hurt you, but you know—
if one loves, the pain is soon forgotten. And you do love me!

'Thank you! Yes! I thank you for that love of yours,

because it is stamped on my memory like a sweet dream, long remembered after waking; because I will remember for ever that moment when you opened your heart to me like a brother, and so generously accepted my own, crushed as it was, to guard, cherish, and heal ... If you forgive me, the memory of you will be exalted within me into an eternal sense of gratitude towards you which will never be erased from my soul ... I will preserve that memory, be ever faithful to it, never betray it or my heart: it is too steadfast. Yesterday indeed, it returned so swiftly to the one to whom if forever belongs.

'We shall meet, you will visit us, you won't desert us, you will always be my friend and brother ... And when you see me, you will give me your hand ... yes? You will give it to me, you have forgiven me, haven't you? You love me *as before*?

'Ah, do love me, do not forsake me, because I love you so much at this moment, because I am worthy of your love, because I deserve it ... my dear friend! Next week I am getting married to him. He came back as a lover, he had never forgotten me ... Don't be angry that I have written about him. But I want to come with him to see you; you will take to him, won't you?

'Forgive us, remember and love your

Nastenka.'

I read the letter over and over for a long time as tears welled up in my eyes. At length it dropped from my hands and I covered my face.

'Deary!' Matryona began.

'What is it, old woman?'

'Those cobwebs, I've got rid of them all off the ceiling; you can get married, or invite guests round, just the time for it ...'

I glanced at Matryona ... She was still a sprightly, *young* old woman, but I don't know why, she suddenly seemed to me stooped and decrepit, her eyes dimmed, her face wrinkled ... I don't know why, but my room had aged just like the old woman. The walls and floor had faded, everything had grown dingy; there were more cobwebs than ever. I don't know why, but when I glanced out of the window, it seemed that the house opposite had also grown decrepit and dingy, the stucco on the columns peeling and dropping off, the cornices darkened and cracked, the dark-ochre walls patchy and mottled . . .

Either a darting ray of sunshine had suddenly vanished behind a rain-cloud and rendered everything dull before my eyes, or perhaps the entire perspective of my future had flashed before me, so miserable and uninviting, and I saw myself just as I was now, fifteen years on, growing old, in the same room, alone as now with the same old Matryona, grown not a whit more intelligent over the years.

As if I would nurse my resentment, Nastenka! As if I would drive a dark cloud across your bright, serene happiness, as if I would inflict misery on your heart with my bitter reproaches, wound it with covert pangs and make it beat anxiously in your moment of bliss, or crush even one of those tender blossoms woven into your dark curls, when you go with him to the altar . . . Oh, never, never! May your sky be clear, may your sweet smile be bright and serene, may you be blessed for the moment of bliss and happiness, which you gave to another, a lonely, grateful heart!

God in heaven! A whole moment of bliss! Is that not sufficient even for a man's entire life? . . .

A GENTLE CREATURE

A GENTLE CREATURE

A GENTLE CREATURE

A FANTASTIC STORY

FROM THE AUTHOR

I MUST apologize to my readers for giving them a story on this occasion in place of the usual 'Diary' format. But I really have been busy on this tale for the better part of a month. At all events, I crave the reader's indulgence.

Now as to the story itself. I have entitled it 'fantastic', though I personally regard it as being extremely realistic. Nevertheless, there is an element of the fantastic here, embodied in the form of the narrative itself, which I feel it necessary to explain in advance.

The fact is that this is not a story and not diary jottings either. Picture to yourselves a husband, whose wife has committed suicide some hours previously by throwing herself from a window, and is now lying on the table. He is in shock and has not yet managed to collect his scattered thoughts. He walks about his apartment, trying to make sense of what has happened, to 'bring his thoughts into focus'. Moreover he is a confirmed hypochondriac, of the sort that talk to themselves. So here he is talking to himself, going over the business, trying to make sense of it. Notwithstanding the apparent coherence of his words, he contradicts himself several times, both in logic and in the emotional sense. He tries to vindicate himself and put the blame on her, then launches out on irrelevant explanations: here we see his coarseness of mind and heart, as well as the depth of his feelings. Gradually he really does make sense of what has occurred in his own terms and 'brings his thoughts into focus'. A series of recollections at length lead him inexorably to *the truth*; that truth inevitably exalts his mind and heart. Towards the end, even the tone of the story alters, compared with its confused beginning. The truth is revealed to the wretched man in terms which are sufficiently clear and unambiguous, at least for him.

So much for the plot. Of course, the narrative takes place over a number of hours, by fits and starts, no consistency of form: at times he talks to himself, at times he addresses an unseen auditor, a sort of judge. That's how it always is in real life. If a stenographer could have overheard him and taken notes as he spoke, the result might have been somewhat rougher and less polished than I have here presented it, but I do believe that the psychological sequence would remain one and the same. It is this notion of a supposed stenographer noting everything down (to be subsequently polished by me), that I term fantastic in this tale. But something of the sort has been permitted in art more than once before now: Victor Hugo for example, in his masterpiece *Le Dernier Jour d'un condamné*, employed virtually the same device, and although he did not use a stenographer to be sure, he allowed himself a still greater implausibility in assuming that a condemned man would be able (and have the time) to make notes, not only on his last day, but even during his last hour, and quite literally his final moment. Still, on the other hand, had he not allowed himself this flight of fancy, the work itself—the most realistic and truthful of any that he wrote—would not now exist.

CHAPTER ONE

1. Who I Was and Who She Was

. . . So as long as she's here, everything's still all right: I can go over and look at her any time; but tomorrow they'll be taking her away and how on earth will I manage on my own? At the moment she's in the room on a table, two card-tables put together, but tomorrow the coffin arrives, white, white *gros de Naples*,* still, where was I . . . I keep pacing about trying to make sense of all this. I've been trying to make sense of it for six hours now and I still can't get my thoughts into focus. The thing is, I keep on pacing and pacing about . . . This is how it happened. I'll just tell it in order (order!). Ladies and gentlemen, I'm a long way from being a literary man, as you can well see, but be that as it may, I will tell it as far as I understand it. In fact, that's the horrible thing about it for me—I understand it all!

If you want to know, I mean if I start from the very beginning, she used to come to me to pawn articles, as simple as that, to finance an advertisement in *The Voice*—something on the lines of governess, willing to travel, give lessons at people's homes, and so on and so forth. That was at the very beginning and naturally I didn't differentiate between her and the others; she used to come along like the rest, well, you know. Then I did begin to take notice of her. She was a fair-haired, delicate creature, medium tall; she was always ill at ease with me, awkward somehow (I fancy she was like that with everybody she didn't know, and to her of course I was no different from anyone else, as a man I mean, not a pawnbroker). As soon as she got her money, she would turn about and leave immediately. And not a word spoken. The others used to argue, insist, haggle for more; she never did, just took what was offered . . . I fancy I'm getting things out of order . . . Yes; the first thing that struck me was the type of thing she used to bring in: little silver-gilt earrings, a trashy little medallion—not worth two kopeks any of it. She was well aware they were only worth coppers, but I could tell by her face that to her they were precious—in fact they were all that remained to her of her father and mother, as I afterwards learned. Only once did I presume to smile at these trinkets of hers. I mean, I never let myself do that, you see, I maintain a gentlemanly front with the public: few words, polite and formal. 'Discipline, discipline, always discipline.'* But, all of a sudden, she had ventured to bring the remnants (I mean literally) of an old jacket lined with rabbit fur, I just couldn't help coming out with some witticism. Ye gods, did she flare up! She had big blue wistful eyes, but how they flashed! She uttered no word, however, just gathered up the 'remnants' and went off. It was at that point that I took *special* notice of her for the first time and started thinking about her in that way, I mean in a special sort of way. Yes: I also remember what struck me, my chief impression if you like, what summed it all up: it was that she was terribly young, so young you'd have taken her for 14. Yet in fact she was actually three months off 16. Still, that's not what I wanted to say, that wasn't what I meant by summing her up. She turned up again the following day. I found out later that she'd been to Dobronravov and Mozer* with that jacket of hers, but they take nothing but gold and wouldn't discuss the matter. I did once accept a precious stone from her (rubbishy, you know) and when I came to think about it afterwards, I was surprised: I don't accept anything apart from gold and silver myself, but I'd let her pawn a stone. That was the second thought I had about her at the time, I remember that.

On this occasion, coming back from Mozer I mean, she brought an amber cigar-holder—not a bad little article, a collector's item, but valueless as far as we were concerned, because we only deal in gold. Since this was after the previous day's *revolt* I received her formally. With me that takes the form of coldness. However, as I gave her two roubles, I couldn't help adding with a hint of irritation: 'You know, I'm only doing this because *it's you*. Mozer wouldn't accept a thing like this.' I made a point of stressing the words 'it's you', giving them a *special meaning*. I was being spiteful. She flared up again on hearing 'it's you', but held her peace and took the money without flinging it back—that's what poverty does to you! But did she flare up! I knew I'd touched a nerve. After she had gone, I asked myself suddenly: was it really worth two roubles to triumph over her? Heh, heh, heh! I remember asking myself twice over: 'Was it worth it? Was it worth it?' And laughed as I answered my own question in the affirmative. I enjoyed myself no end at the time. There was nothing ill-natured about it, though: I had a purpose, something in mind; I meant to test her because certain notions touching her had occurred to me. That was the third *special* kind of thought I had about her.

. . . So that's how it all started. Naturally, I immediately began finding out everything I could about her indirectly, and awaited her arrival with a special sense of anticipation. I certainly had a premonition that she would be coming back soon. When she did arrive, I launched into a polite conversation with extreme courtesy. I am after all a man of some breeding and I do have manners. Ahem. I divined at once that she was a gentle and kindly creature. Gentle and kindly creatures don't put up much resistance and, though they may not reveal much of themselves, they have no idea of how to evade a conversation: they are sparing in their replies but they do reply, and the longer it goes on, the more you learn, but you have to keep at it, if that's what you're after. Naturally she didn't explain anything at the time. That bit about *The Voice* and the rest of it I found out later on. She was advertising with the last of her resources then, proudly at first: 'Governess, willing to travel, conditions of employment should be sent in sealed envelope', then later: 'Willing to take on anything, teaching, lady's companion, housekeeping, nursing, able to sew' and so on and so forth, the usual kind of thing! Naturally, all this was added to the advertisement in gradual stages and towards the end, when despair was setting in, there came 'no salary required, board only'. No, she couldn't find a post! I made up my mind to test her one last time: I suddenly picked up that day's *Voice* and showed her an advertisement: 'Young lady, orphan, seeks a post as governess, preferably with a middle-aged widower. Can assist with housekeeping.'

'There, you see, that was in the paper this morning and she probably found a job by evening. Now that's the way to advertise!'

She flared up again, again her eyes blazed as she turned and went out. I was much taken with that. Actually, by that time I was supremely confident about the whole business and had no qualms at all: nobody would take those cigar-holders of hers. And anyway she'd run out of those too. So it turned out, two days later in she comes, all pale and full of nerves; I guessed that something had happened at home, and so it had. I'll explain presently what that was, but I would just like to recall how I suddenly put on a bit of style and rose in her estimation. This was the notion that suddenly came to me. The point was she had brought me this icon (nerved herself to do it!). . . Ah, listen, just listen! This was when it really began, I've been getting it all mixed up . . . The thing is now I want to recall everything, every tiny point, every detail. I keep wanting to get my thoughts into focus and—I just can't, and then those details, details . . .

An icon of the Madonna. Madonna and child, domestic, a family, ancient, silver-gilt mounting, worth say six roubles. I could see she treasured it; she was pawning the whole thing, mounting and all. I told her it would be better to detach the mounting and take the icon away, it was an icon after all.

'Surely you're not forbidden to accept it?'

'No, not forbidden, it's just that perhaps you . . .'

'All right, detach the mounting.'

'I'll tell you what, I won't take it off, I'll put it over there in the icon case', I said, after a moment's thought, 'along with the other icons under the lamp' (the lamp had been kept permanently lit since I opened the office), 'and you can have ten roubles and there's all about it.'

'I don't need ten, just give me five. I assure you I'll redeem it.'

'You don't want ten? The icon's worth that', I added, noting that her eyes had flashed again. She said nothing. I took out five roubles for her.

'No need to look down on people, I've been in similar straits myself, even worse in fact, yes indeed, and if you see me now in this occupation . . . well, it's after coming through a good deal . . .'

'You're getting your own back against society, is that it?' she broke in. Still, there was a deal of innocence in the tart mockery (generalized I mean, because at that time she certainly did not differentiate between me and anyone else, so the effect was inoffensive). 'Aha', thought I. 'So that's the kind of girl you are, your true character emerges, you're one of the "new tendency".'

'You see', I put in at once, half-jocular, half-enigmatic, 'I . . . I am part of that part of the whole which would work evil but engenders good instead . . .'

She shot a swift glance at me. Her keen curiosity had much that was childlike.

'Just a moment . . . What was that idea? Where does it come from? I've heard it somewhere . . .'

'Don't rack your brains, it's Mephistopheles introducing himself to Faust. You've read *Faust*?'

'Not . . . properly.'

'Not read it at all you mean. You should. However, I can see something of a sneer on your lips again. Please don't suppose I am so deficient in taste as to glorify my role as pawnbroker by introducing myself as Mephistopheles. Once a pawnbroker, always a pawnbroker. I'm aware of that, miss.'

'You're rather a strange man . . . I wasn't intending to say anything of the sort . . .'

What she implied was: I didn't expect you to be an educated man. She didn't say it, but I knew that was what she was thinking; I'd made no end of an impression.

'You see', I remarked, 'a man can do good whatever career he follows. I exclude myself of course, one might say I do nothing of the kind, but . . .'

'Of course one can do good in any job', she said, with a swift and penetrating glance at me. 'Any job at all', she added abruptly. Ah, I remember, I remember all those moments! I would also add, that when young people, those sweet young things, try to come out with something clever and perceptive, their faces show only too frankly and naïvely that 'now I'm telling you something clever and perceptive', not out of vanity like the rest of us; no, you can see that she places enormous value on it all and believes and respects it, thinking that you hold it in the same high regard. Ah, sincerity! That's how they lay us low. And how delightful it was in her!

I remember it all, I've forgotten nothing! After she had gone out, I immediately came to a decision. That very day I went about my final enquiries and found out what else there was to know about her, all the latest ins and outs; I had elicited all the details of her earlier life from Lukeriya, who worked for them at the time and whom I had bribed some days earlier. Those details had been so horrifying that I simply don't understand how she could laugh as she had done just now, or become curious about Mephistopheles' words when she herself was in such a dreadful situation. But—there's youth for you! That was precisely what I thought about her then with pride and gladness, because there was high-mindedness, as if to say: even on the brink of disaster, Goethe's words shine out. Young people always have at least a dash of this high-mindedness, even if it's wrong-headed. But it's really her I'm talking about, just her. The point was, I was already beginning to look on her as *mine* and had no doubts about my power. You know, that's a really sensual feeling, when you have no doubts at all.

But what's the matter with me? If I go on like this, when am I going to get it all in focus? Quick about it—this is all beside the point, God!

ii. A Proposal of Marriage

THE 'details' I had learned about her I can recount in a very few words: her father and mother had died a considerable time before, three years previously, and she had been left in the hands of some disorganized aunts of hers. And that's putting it mildly. One aunt was a widow, with a numerous family, six children in descending order of age. The other was an old maid, awful woman. They were both awful. The father had been an official but only in the clerical grade, and his title was non-hereditary. In a word: the situation was made for me. I had appeared as it were from some higher world: I was a retired staff captain from a crack regiment, a hereditary nobleman, of independent means, so forth. As for the pawnbroking business, the aunts could only have a respectful attitude towards that. She had been a slave to those aunties for three years, but had nevertheless passed some sort of exam, contrived to pass it, found leisure indeed to pass it despite her pitiless daily round of toil, and that certainly was a good indication of aspirations towards the lofty and noble on her part. After all, why did I intend to marry her? Still, never mind me, that can wait . . . It's irrelevant anyway!

She tutored the aunties' children, made underclothes, and ended up not only washing clothes but scrubbing floors too, with that chest of hers. They even used to beat her, just like that, and begrudged her a crust of bread. In the end they were considering selling her. Ugh! I'll omit the sordid details. Later she told me all about it. The fat shopkeeper next door, owner of two grocery stores besides, had been keeping an eye on all this for a year or more. He had buried two wives already and was on the look-out for a third, so he was running the rule over her: 'She's a quiet sort of girl', thought he, 'grown up in poverty; I'll marry her for the sake of the children.' And he did indeed have children. He started making advances, and opened negotiations with the aunts. He was a man of 50, and she was horrified. That was when she started frequenting my premises to finance the advertisements in the *The Voice*. At length, she asked her aunts to allow her just the briefest time to think the matter over. They gave her precisely that and no more; they kept on at her: 'We don't know where the next meal is coming from ourselves, and that's without an extra mouth to feed.' I was well aware that all this was going on and that same day, after the morning's incident, I made my decision. That evening, the grocer turned up with a fifty-kopek pound of sweets from the shop; she was sitting with him when I summoned Lukeriya from the kitchen and told her to whisper that I was at the front gate and had something very urgent to tell her. I was feeling pleased with myself. In fact I had been in a frightfully good mood all that day.

There and then, by the gate, with Lukeriya present, I

explained to her, astonished as she was by my summons, that I would regard it as my good fortune and an honour ... Secondly, she wasn't to be too surprised at my manner and the fact that we were at the front gate: I was a blunt individual, I said, and was well aware of how matters stood. Blunt was no more than the truth. Well, never mind about that. I spoke with due decorum, demonstrating thereby that I was well bred, but also with a touch of originality, which was what really mattered. Well, is that so dreadful a confession? I intend to sit in judgement on myself and am so doing. I am bound to speak pro and contra, and am so doing. Afterwards I recalled the scene with positive pleasure, though that was silly too: I declared bluntly, without a trace of embarrassment, that firstly I had no great talent, wasn't especially clever, perhaps not especially good-natured either, rather a cheap sort of egoist (I remember that expression, I'd thought it up on the way there and was much taken with it), and that it was eminently possible that I possessed a good many defects in other areas too. All this was delivered with a peculiar kind of pride—everybody knows the technique. Of course, after nobly declaring my shortcomings, I had sufficient good taste not to launch into a catalogue of my virtues, as it might be: 'But, on the other hand, I am this, that or the other.' I could see that as yet she was horribly nervous, but I didn't cushion the effect of this, far from it; observing her alarm, I deliberately intensified it. I said plainly that she would have enough to eat, but as for fine clothes, theatres, dancing—there would be none of that, except possibly later on when I had achieved my aim. I was getting quite carried away with this harsh tone I had adopted. I added, as casually as I could, that if I had undertaken this business, running a pawnbroker's office I mean, it was because I had only one end in view; there was, so to speak, a certain circumstance ... But after all, I did have the right to speak in this way: I really did have such an end in view, and the circumstance did exist. Just a moment, ladies and gentlemen, all my life I have been the first to detest this pawnbroking business, but in actual fact, though it may be absurd to be talking to myself in enigmatic phrases, I was indeed 'taking it out on society', I was, I really was! So that her gibe of that morning about me avenging myself was unjustified. You see, what I mean is, if I had come straight out with the words: 'Yes, I'm taking it out on society', she would have burst out laughing, the way she had done that morning, and the whole thing would have been an absurdity. Well then, an oblique hint and an enigmatic phrase were enough, it seemed, to beguile her imagination. Besides, by now I was absolutely certain of myself: at all events, I knew, of course, that the fat shopkeeper was more repulsive to her than I was, and that as I stood by the gate, I appeared in the guise of liberator. I was fully aware of that. Ah yes, man understands his contemptible actions all too well! But were they contemptible, though? How can a man be judged in a case like this? Didn't I love her even then?

Wait: naturally, I said not so much as a word to her about being her benefactor; on the contrary, very much the contrary: 'It is I who am in receipt of any favour, not *you*.' I went so far as to utter it aloud, I couldn't help it, and no doubt it sounded rather silly, as I noticed the fleeting ghost of a smile on her face. But overall I emerged the victor. Wait a moment: if I have to bring all this filth up, I'll include my final swinish trick: I was standing and it crossed my mind: you're tall, slim, well bred—and really, without boasting, not bad looking. That was the notion I was toying with. Naturally, she said 'yes' then and there. But ... but I have to add that as she stood there by the gate, she thought it over for a long time before saying 'yes'. She pondered and pondered so long I was on the point of asking: 'Well, what then?' and couldn't help adding a bit of a flourish: 'Well, what's it to be then, miss?'

'Wait, I'm thinking.'

And what a grave little face she had; I should have read it even then! But my reaction was to take offence: 'Surely, I thought, she wasn't taking time to choose between a businessman and myself? Ah, how little I understood at the time! I understood precisely nothing at the time! I haven't realized it until today. I remember Lukeriya running out after me as I was leaving, and stopping me on the road as she gasped: 'God will reward you, sir, for taking our dear young lady, but don't tell her that, she's a proud one.'

Proud, eh? Well, I thought, I'm fond of proud little girls. The proud ones are especially nice when ... well, when you're confident of your power over them, eh? Ah, you sordid, blundering individual! Oh, how pleased I was with myself! You know, as she stood there by the gate considering whether to say 'yes', I was astonished, you know, that she might be entertaining some such notion as: 'If I'm to be unhappy in any event, would it not be better to choose the worst one straight away, the fat shopkeeper, and let him beat me to death when he's drunk, sooner the better?' Eh? What say you, could she have been thinking that?

Even now I don't understand, even now it's all a mystery to me. I said just now that she might have been thinking that way; to choose the worse of two calamities, the shopkeeper that is. But who was the worse for her then—the grocer or me? The tradesman or the Goethe-quoting pawnbroker? Now there's a question! What question? You can't make sense of that either: the answer is lying on that table and you say 'question'! Well, never mind about me! I'm totally irrelevant ... Incidentally, what is it to me now whether I'm irrelevant or not? That really is completely beyond me. Better turn in. I've got a headache ...

III. The Noblest of Men, but I Don't Believe that Myself

I COULDN'T get to sleep. How could I with that pulse pounding away inside my head? I keep wanting to assimilate all that filth. Ah, the filth! The filth I extricated her from back then! I mean she must have realized it, appreciated what I was doing! There were various notions that appealed to me at the time, that I was 41, for instance, while she was barely 16. The thought entranced me, that sense of disparity, most delightful that, most delightful.

For instance, I wanted a wedding *à l'anglaise*, just the two of us in other words, with only the two witnesses, one of them

Lukeriya, then off on the train for Moscow, say (where I had some business to see to, incidentally), and a fortnight or so in a hotel. She was opposed to this, wouldn't countenance it, so I was forced to go and see the aunts, treating them with courtesy as if they were relatives I was taking her away from. I yielded and the aunts received their due. I went so far as to present the creatures with a hundred roubles apiece and promised more, not letting on to her of course, so as not to upset her with the shabbiness of the proceeding. The aunts melted at once. There was an argument about the trousseau: she had nothing, almost literally, but then she didn't want anything. However, I managed to persuade her that to have nothing at all was out of the question, and I bought the trousseau myself—who else was to do it for her? Well, never mind about me. I did manage to get some of my ideas across to her, nevertheless, so that at least she was aware of them. I was in too much of a hurry perhaps. Anyway, the main thing is that right from the start, however much she tried to restrain herself, she would come rushing to me with love, greeting me ecstatically when I came back in the evenings, prattling away (that enchanting prattle of innocence!) about her childhood, or when she was a baby, about her parents' house, her father and mother. But I was quick to pour cold water over all this rapture. That was the point of my idea. I responded to these transports with silence, a benevolent silence, of course . . . but all the same she soon came to see that we were different and that I was an enigma—the very thing I was striving for! Why, that could have been the precise reason, to construct an enigma I mean, that I embarked on the whole stupid undertaking! First came discipline—it was in a spirit of discipline that I brought her into my house. Anyway, there I was, walking about quite happily, as I devised my complete system. Oh, it took shape by itself, effortlessly. Nor could it have been otherwise. I was forced to devise this system by circumstances beyond my control—why, what on earth am I doing disparaging myself! The system was genuine. No, hear me out, if a man is to be judged, let it be with full possession of the facts . . . Listen.

How to begin then, because this is very difficult. When you

start justifying yourself, that's the difficult part. What I mean
is, young people, say, despise money—so I immediately
began emphasizing money matters; I laid great stress on
money. I kept on about it so much that she began saying less
and less. She would open her large eyes wide, listening,
staring, and holding her peace. Young people are high-
minded, the good ones among them I mean, high-minded
and impulsive, but they are intolerant; the least thing unto-
ward and it's contempt. What I wanted was broadmindedness,
I wanted to inculcate a broad outlook directly into her heart,
instil it into her basic attitudes, you know what I mean? Let's
take a vulgar example: how could I, for instance, explain my
pawnbroking business to someone of her character? Naturally, I didn't put it as bluntly as that, otherwise it would have
looked as if I were apologizing for the pawnshop; no, I made
it a matter of pride, as it were, deploying an eloquent silence.
I'm an expert at this. I've been doing it all my life and lived
through whole tragedies in silence. Oh, I have been wretched
too, you know! I have been rejected by one and all, rejected
and forgotten, and no one, no one at all knows of it! And all
of a sudden this 16-year-old had got hold of some snippets
about me from disreputable folk and thought she knew
everything—meanwhile the essential truth lay hidden in the
breast of this man! I maintained my silence, especially,
especially with her, right up till yesterday—why did I do that?
Simply because I have my pride. I wanted her to discover for
herself, without my intervention, and not from disreputable
folks' stories—to *divine for herself* the truth about this man
and comprehend him! In accepting her into my house I
required total respect. I wanted her to kneel before me in
prayer for my sufferings—and I merited that. Oh, I have
always had my pride, all or nothing, that was me. Precisely
because I have never countenanced half measures where
happiness was concerned, because I wanted everything—I
was compelled to act precisely in the way I did then, as if to
say: 'Think it out and judge for yourself!' because, you will
agree, if I had started explaining and prompting her myself,
cringed and solicited respect—it would be tantamount to

begging alms ... Still ... still, why on earth am I going on about this?

Stupid, stupid, stupid! With pitiless bluntness (and I emphasize the word 'pitiless') I briefly explained to her that the high-mindedness of young people was all very fine but it wasn't worth a brass farthing. Why so? Because it was cheaply come by, not gained through living experience, it was all, so to speak, 'first impressions of existence'*—let's see you get down to a bit of work! Generosity that costs nothing is always easy, even sacrificing your life—even that is cheap because it is just the fire in the blood and an excess of energy,* the passionate desire for the fine gesture! No, take on a high-minded deed which is difficult, quiet, obscure, without outward show, one entailing vilification, one involving much sacrifice and not a hint of glory—where you, the illustrious man, the most upright person on earth, are held up to one and all as contemptible—now then, just you try doing that. No indeed, you'd have none of it! But as for me, I've spent my entire life accomplishing such a feat. At first she argued with me, indeed she did, then began to quieten down, altogether in fact, though her eyes were enormously wide as she listened, big, big eyes they were, all attention. And ... and besides, I suddenly caught her smile, mistrustful, silent, unpleasant. It was with that smile on her face that I had conducted her into my house. It's also true, of course, that she had nowhere else to go ...

iv. Plans and More Plans

Which of us started it?

Neither. It began of its own accord right at the outset. I said that I brought her into my house in a spirit of discipline, but right from the beginning I softened that approach. Even before the wedding, it had been explained to her that she would have the job of taking in pledges and handing out the money, and (note this) she said nothing at the time, did she? What's more, she set to work with a positive will. Well of course, the apartment, the furniture—everything stayed as it was. There are two rooms: one a sizeable drawing-room, with the counter partitioned off, and the other, also fair-sized, is our living-room and bedroom combined. My furniture is shabby—even the aunts were better off in that regard. My icon case with the little lamp is in the drawing-room where the cash office is; I have my bookcase with a few volumes in it, and my chest, to which I keep the keys; and there's a bed of course, tables, and chairs. Before we were married, I told her that to support me, herself, and Lukeriya, whom I had lured into my household, daily outgoings on food were not to exceed one rouble: I told her I had to have thirty thousand roubles in three years' time, otherwise I'd never make my fortune. She made no difficulties about this, but I increased the expense allowance by thirty kopeks unprompted. The same went for the theatre. I had told my prospective bride that there would be no theatres, but nevertheless decided to go there once a month, with a proper seat in the stalls. We went together three times and saw *The Pursuit of Happiness*, and *Songbirds*,* I think it was. (Who cares! Who cares!) We went in silence and returned in silence. Why, oh why did we get into this habit of silence right from the start? After all, there was no quarrelling to begin with, but there was still silence. I do remember, however, that she would keep glancing furtively at me; as soon as I noticed this, I intensified the silence. It was really me that insisted on silence, not her. On her part, there were one or two impulsive outbursts when she would run to embrace me, but since these were morbid and hysterical, and what I needed from her was firmly based happiness, combined with respect, I received them coldly. And I was right to do so: after each such outburst there would be a quarrel the following day.

Well, there were no quarrels actually, but there was silence and, more and more often, a bold look on her part. 'Rebellion and independence' is what it was, but she couldn't carry it off. Yes, that meek face was beginning to get ever bolder. If you can believe it, she was starting to find me repulsive, I could watch it happening. And the fact that she had fits of losing her temper was incontestable. For instance, how could she suddenly start sneering at our straitened circumstances—she who had come up from filth and poverty, after scrubbing floors indeed! I mean, it wasn't poverty, it was economy; there was an ample supply of what was essential—linen for example, and cleanliness. Formerly, I had always fancied that women found cleanliness in a man attractive. Still, it wasn't the poverty she meant, it was my supposed miserliness about the household budget: 'He's got it all planned out, has he, showing me how strong-minded he is.' All of a sudden, she turned down the theatre visits. And that derisive look came more and more often ... and I emphasized my silence more and more.

Justify my actions then? The main thing in all this was the pawnbroking business. Allow me to point out, sirs, that I knew that a woman, especially one of 16, has no option but to sumbit totally to a man. Women possess no originality, that's—that's an axiom, even now, even now I regard that as an axiom! Never mind what's lying out there in the drawing-room: the truth is the truth, Mill* himself can't argue with that! But a loving woman, ah, a loving woman, idolizes even the vices, even the wicked actions of her beloved. He himself couldn't devise the justifications for his evil conduct that she can find for him. It bespeaks generosity but not originality. Lack of originality has been the undoing of women. So why, I repeat, why point to that table? Do you mean to say what lies on that table is original? Oho!

Listen: I was certain she loved me at that time. Why, she still used to throw her arms round my neck even then. She loved me, in other words, or rather, desired so to do. Yes, that's how it was: she wanted to love me, sought to love me. The thing is, really, that there was no sort of villainy on my part for her to drum up justification for. You say 'pawnbroker', like everyone else does. Well, what if I am? It follows there must be a reason if the most high-minded of men turns pawnbroker. You see, ladies and gentlemen, there are notions ... I mean, do you see, if you come out with certain ideas in so many words, they sound awfully silly. You feel ignominious. Why is that? No reason at all. Because we're all worthless and can't bear to hear the truth, or something of the sort. I said 'most high-minded of men' just now. It sounds absurd, and yet that's how it really was. It's actually true, the honest truth! Yes, *I had the right* to seek to earn my living and open this pawnshop. I thought: 'You, people, have spurned me, you have driven me away with silent contempt. You have responded to my passionate impulse towards you with an injury that shall last my lifetime. Consequently I am now within my rights to wall myself off from you, put together these thirty thousand roubles and end my life somewhere in the Crimea, on the south coast, among the mountains and vineyards, on my own estate, purchased with that thirty thousand, and above all, far away from all of you, but with no malice towards you; with an ideal in my soul and the woman of my heart, a family, if God so sends—and a source of succour to the neighbouring peasants.' Of course, it's all right for me to say this about myself now, but what could have sounded sillier if I had described all that to her out loud? Hence the proud reticence, that's why we sat in silence. Because what would she have comprehended? Only 16, the first flush of youth, what could she possibly have understood of my self-justifications, my sufferings? What you have is simplistic ignorance of life, callow, vulgar convictions, the night blindness of 'splendid hearts', whereas what mattered was the pawnshop and—*basta!** And surely I was no scoundrel in the business, surely she could see how I behaved and whether I overcharged? Ah, how fearful is the truth upon this earth! This delight, this gentle creature, this heaven—she was a tyrant, the intolerable tyrant and tormentor of my soul! I am denigrating myself if I fail to say that! You think I didn't love her? Who can deny that I loved her? There was an irony here, do you see, a bitter irony of fate and nature! We are accursed, the life of man is altogether accursed! (Mine especially!) Of course I realize now that I went astray somewhere in all this! Things went wrong. It had all been crystal clear, my plan was as plain as day: 'Proud and austere, he suffers in silence, needing no one's moral solace.' That's the way it was, I wasn't lying, I wasn't lying! 'She will come to see it herself, that there was greatness of soul involved, but she has not been able to recognize it for what it was—and when she eventually does divine the truth, she will esteem it tenfold and fall to her knees on the ground, her hands clasped in prayer.' Such was the plan. But I forgot or overlooked something. There was some matter I failed to perform. Still, enough, enough of that. And whom to ask forgiveness? What's done is done. Brace up man, have some pride! It's not your fault! . . .

Very well, I shall tell the truth, I'm not afraid to face up to it: it's *her* fault, *her* fault! . . .

v. The Gentle Creature Rebels

THE squabbling started when she took it into her head all of a sudden to over-value articles, and on one or two occasions was disposed to enter into an argument with me on the subject. I declined. However, at this juncture, the captain's widow turned up.

The old woman had come along with a medallion—a gift from her late husband, a souvenir, you know the sort of thing. I gave her thirty roubles. She started whimpering plaintively, begging me to take good care of the article—which we always do of course. Well, anyway, she came in five days later wanting to exchange it for a bracelet not worth eight roubles; I refused, naturally. She must have caught something in my wife's expression at the time, because she came when I wasn't there and my wife exchanged the medallion.

I found out about it the same day and began to talk to her mildly, but in a firm and logical manner. She was sitting on the bed, regarding the floor, scuffing her right toe on the carpet (a habit of hers); a disagreeable smile played about her lips. Then, without raising my voice in the least, I pointed out that the money was *mine*, that I had the right to regard life through *my* eyes—and that when I had invited her into my house, I had not concealed anything of this.

She suddenly bounded to her feet, quivering in every fibre and—can you imagine—started stamping her feet at me; it was a wild animal, a fit of some kind, it was a wild animal in a seizure. I froze in astonishment: I had never expected an outburst like this. But I retained my composure, I didn't even move; I declared there and then, still in my previous unruffled tone, that henceforth I would not be allowing her to participate in my business activities. She burst out laughing in my face and left the apartment.

The point is, she had no right to leave the apartment. Nowhere without me, that had been the agreement before our marriage. Towards evening she returned; I said not a word.

First thing next day, she went out again, and again the day after that. I shut up shop and went off to the aunts. I had broken with them directly after the wedding—no invitations either way. It turned out that she hadn't been with them. They heard me out inquisitively and then laughed in my face: 'Serves you right', they said. But I had anticipated their laughter. I at once bribed the younger aunt, the unmarried one, with a hundred roubles plus twenty-five in advance. She came to see me a couple of days later: 'There's a former fellow officer of yours mixed up in this, a Lieutenant Yefimovich', she said. I was extremely taken aback. This Yefimovich had caused me more harm in the regiment than anyone else. Once or twice, a month before, being impervious to shame, he had called in at the counter, supposedly about pawning something and, as I recall, my wife and he had started laughing together. At the time I had gone over to him and told him not to presume to call, bearing in mind what had passed between us; but no thought of anything like this had crossed my mind, I merely thought he was being insolent. Now here was this aunt informing me out of the blue that they had already arranged to meet, and that the whole affair was being set in train by an old former acquaintance of the aunts—Yuliya Samsonovna, a colonel's widow to boot. 'It's her', said she, 'that your wife now goes to see.'

I shall not dwell on the matter. It cost me between two and three hundred roubles altogether, but within two days it was arranged that I should stand in the next room, with the door ajar, and overhear the first private rendezvous between my wife and Yefimovich. As a harbinger of this, a brief—but to me all-too-significant—scene was played out between the two of us.

She had returned towards evening and sat herself down on the bed, regarding me mockingly. She began tapping her foot on the carpet. As I watched her, it occurred to me that over this past month or, more precisely, this past fortnight, she had been acting wholly out of character—assuming a totally opposite guise, even: an obstreperous, belligerent creature had emerged—I won't say brazen, but wild and deliberately courting trouble. Asking for it. Her essential meekness, however, was hampering her. When a girl like that starts to get out of hand, no matter how much she kicks over the traces, it's still obvious that she's only egging herself on, driving herself, and that she really finds it impossible to overcome her own modesty and sense of shame. That's why such women sometimes overstep the mark in a way that seems incredible even as you observe it. Those hardened in depravity, on the other hand, always play things down; their actions are more vile, but are clothed in propriety and a show of decency, which claims a superiority over your own.

'Is it true you were dismissed from your regiment because you backed out of a duel?' she asked abruptly, right out of the blue, her eyes glittering.

'Yes; the verdict of the officers' court was that I should be required to leave the regiment, although I had already applied to resign my commission before that.'

'Dismissed on grounds of cowardice?'

'Yes, that was their verdict. But I did not refuse the duel from motives of cowardice, but because I did not wish to submit myself to their despotic verdict and call a man out to a duel when I did not consider myself insulted. You know', I couldn't help adding, 'to take action against tyranny of that sort and accept all the consequences meant demonstrating a great deal more courage than fighting a duel.'

I couldn't hold back. With that sentence I found myself embarked on a course of self-justification; and that was just what she wanted, this new humiliation of mine. She burst into malicious laughter.

'And is it true that you wandered the streets of Petersburg like a beggar, cadging coppers and sleeping under billiard tables?'

'I did spend nights in the Vyazemsky House* on the Haymarket. Yes, it's true; my life after the army contained much that was shameful and degrading, though not in the moral sense, because I detested my own actions even at the time. It was merely a degradation of mind and will, prompted by despair at my situation. But that passed . . .'

'Ah, now you're a personage—a financier!'

A hit at the pawnbroking, you see. But I had myself well in hand by now. I could see that she was avid for humiliating explanations from me and—I declined to give them. A customer opportunely rang the bell at this moment and I went out to him in the drawing-room. Afterwards, an hour later, when she had abruptly got herself ready to go out, she halted in front of me and said:

'You didn't tell me any of this before the wedding, did you?'

I made no reply, and she left.

And so, the following day, I stood behind the door and listened to my fate being decided. I carried a revolver in my pocket. She was dressed up and sitting at the table, while Yefimovich was posturing in front of her. Well now, what occurred (I think this is to my credit) was exactly what I had unconsciously anticipated and presumed would take place. I don't know if I am making myself clear.

What happened was this. I listened for a whole hour and for all of that time I witnessed a duel between a woman of the most exalted nobility and a worldly, dull-witted creature with the soul of a reptile. I was overwhelmed; where, thought I, had this naïve, submissive, reticent girl acquired all this worldly wisdom? The wittiest author of high society comedies could not have devised this scene of mockery, naïve laughter, and the saintly contempt that virtue feels for vice. The brilliance of her words and interjections; the wit of her swift repartee, the truth in her condemnations! Yet at the same time so much that was almost girlishly artless. She laughed in his face in response to his protestations of love, his gestures, his offers. Having arrived with his crude aproach to the matter in hand and not anticipating resistance, he subsided. At first I might have thought she was merely being coy—'the coyness of a sharp-witted if depraved creature, in order to display herself to better advantage'. But not a bit of it, the truth shone forth like the sun, leaving no room for doubt. Inexperienced as she was, she could only have nerved herself to go through with this rendezvous out of a fancied, impulsive hatred of me, but as soon as matters reached a crux, her eyes were instantly opened. Here was a creature rushing hither and yon to find some way, any way, of wounding me, but having once resolved upon such a foul proceeding, found the mess that was involved unendurable. Could Yefimovich or any of those high society creatures really seduce someone so pure and sinless, cherishing her ideal as she did? On the contrary, he merely provoked laughter. The truth ascended from her soul undiminished and her indignation drew forth derision from her heart. I repeat, by the end this clown was totally dazed and sat scowling, barely able to respond; I positively began to worry in case he insulted her out of mean-spirited vengefulness. And I repeat again: to my credit, I heard out this scene almost without astonishment, as if I had encountered something familiar. As if I had gone there in order to encounter it. I had gone believing nothing, no accusation, despite the revolver in my pocket—and that's the truth! And could I really have imagined her behaving other-wise? Wasn't that why I loved and prized her? Wasn't that why I had married her? Oh, of course, at that time I was utterly convinced of her hatred towards me, but I was also convinced of her purity. I brought this scene to a swift conclusion by opening the door. Yefimovich leapt to his feet as I took her arm and invited her to leave with me. He then recovered his wits and burst into peals of ringing laughter.

'Oh, I raise no objection against the holy rites of matri-mony, take her, take her! And look here', he shouted after me, 'although no decent man would fight you, out of respect for your lady I am at your service . . . If you want to risk it . . .'

'You hear that?' I stopped her for a moment on the threshold.

Afterwards, not a word the whole way home. I led her by the arm and she made no resistance. On the contrary, she was horribly shaken, but only till we reached the house. When we arrived, she sat down on a chair and fixed her eyes on me. She was extremely pale; although her lips had at once framed a mocking smile, she looked challengingly at me, grimly solemn, apparently genuinely convinced in those first minutes that I was going to shoot her with the revolver. However, I wordlessly drew the weapon from my pocket and placed it on the table. She looked at me and at the revolver. (Note: she was already familiar with this revolver. I had acquired it and kept it loaded from the day I opened the pawnshop. On starting out in business I had decided against keeping huge dogs or a husky servant like Mozer does, for example. The cook admits my customers. But people in our line of work cannot do without a means of self-defence, just in case, and so I had acquired a loaded revolver. In the first days after she entered my household she had been very curious about this gun and asked me lots of questions about it. I had even explained the mechanism and the way it worked, as well as persuading her to do some target practice. Do note all this.) Ignoring her expression of alarm, I lay down on the bed, half-undressed. I felt very weak; it was already nearly eleven o'clock. She remained sitting in the same place, without budging, for another hour or so, then she doused the candle and went to bed, also without undressing, on the sofa by the wall. This was the first time she had not slept by my side—note that also.

VI. A Dreadful Memory

Now that dreadful memory . . .

I woke up in the morning, some time after seven, I think, and it was almost fully light in the room. I awoke at once into full awareness and swiftly opened my eyes. She was standing by the table holding the revolver. She didn't notice that I had woken up and was watching her. All of a sudden I saw that she had started moving towards me with the gun in her hands. I quickly closed my eyes and pretended to be fast asleep.

She reached the bed and stood above me. I heard every

sound; even though a deathly silence reigned, I could hear that silence. Now there came a spasmodic movement and suddenly I couldn't help involuntarily opening my eyes. She was staring straight at me, directly into my eyes, and the revolver was already at my temple. Our eyes met, but we looked at one another for no more than an instant. I forced my eyes shut again and made an instant resolve, with all the power at my command, that I would not make another move or open my eyes, whatever should await me.

It does actually happen that even someone sound asleep will suddenly open his eyes, even raise his head for a second and look around the room, before laying his head back on the pillow and dropping off to sleep an instant later, with no recollection of the event. When, after encountering her gaze and becoming aware of the revolver at my temple, I then abruptly closed my eyes again and lay motionless, like one in a deep sleep—she might have been forgiven for supposing that I actually was asleep and had seen nothing, particularly as it was beyond belief that, having seen what I had seen, anyone could close their eyes again at such a moment.

Yes, beyond belief. But she could still have divined the actual truth—that too flashed across my mind in the self-same instant. Ah, what a whirlwind of thoughts and sensations raced through my mind in that split second—thank God for the electricity of human thought! In that eventuality (I felt) if she had guessed the truth and realized that I was not asleep, that I had already crushed her by my readiness to accept death, then her hand might well be unsteady now. Her former resolution might disintegrate in the face of this new and extraordinary state of affairs. They say that people standing on high places are somehow tempted to leap down into the abyss of their own accord. In my opinion, a good many murders and suicides have taken place merely because a revolver has been picked up. That too is a kind of abyss, a declivity of forty-five degrees impossible to avoid slithering down, and something inexorably impels you to pull the trigger. But her awareness that I had seen everything, knew everything, and was awaiting death from her in silence—that might stay her on the slope.

The silence persisted, then all of a sudden I sensed by the hair at my temple, the chill touch of metal. You will ask: was I so certain of survival? I will answer, as before God: I had no hope at all, beyond, say, one chance in a hundred. Why on earth was I just accepting my death? I would ask: what use was life to me after a revolver had been raised against me by the creature I adored? Besides which, I knew with all the power of my being, that a struggle was going on between us at that precise moment, a fearful duel of life and death, a duel being fought by that same coward of yesterday, dismissed by his comrades for cowardice. I knew that, and she knew it too, if she had guessed the truth, that I was not asleep.

Perhaps that wasn't the way of it, perhaps I didn't have those thoughts at the time, but it must have been like that all the same, even if unconsciously, because I have done nothing else but think about it every hour of my life since.

But you will pose another question: why on earth did I not save her from her wickedness? Oh, I have put that question to myself a thousand times since—every time, with a chill at my back, I recall that moment. But my soul was in grim despair at that time: I was about to be annihilated myself, so how on earth could I have saved anyone else? And how do you know I wanted to save anyone at the time? Who knows what I might have been feeling?

My mind was seething, however; the seconds passed, the silence was deathly; she was still standing over me—then suddenly I quivered with hope! I swiftly opened my eyes. She was no longer in the room. I rose from the bed: I had conquered—and she had been vanquished for ever!

I went out to the samovar. We always had tea in the main room, and it was she who always poured. I sat down to table without a word and took a glass of tea from her. After about five minutes, I glanced at her. She was dreadfully pale, even paler than the previous day, and she was watching me. Then suddenly—suddenly, seeing that I was looking at her, she smiled wanly, her lips ashen, her eyes looking a hesitant question. 'So, she's still not sure and keeps asking herself: does he know or not, did he see me or did he not?' I turned

my eyes away indifferently. After finishing the tea, I closed
the shop, went to the market, and purchased an iron bedstead
and some screens. Returning home, I ordered the bed to be
set up in the drawing-room and the screens put round it.
This bed was to be hers, but I said not a word to her about
it. Even without words, the bed made her realize that I had
'seen everything and knew everything' and that there could
no longer be any doubt. I left the revolver overnight on the
table as usual. That night she got into the new bed without
saying anything: the marriage was dissolved, she had been
'vanquished but not forgiven'. During the night she became
delirious and by morning fever had set in. She was confined
to bed for six weeks.

CHAPTER TWO

1. A Dream of Pride

LUKERIYA has just announced that she won't be staying with me and that after the mistress has been buried she will be leaving. I have knelt in prayer for five minutes; I wanted to pray for an hour, but I couldn't keep from thinking and thinking, sick thoughts and a sick head—what's the use of praying now? It would be sinful! It's odd, too, I don't feel any inclination to sleep: in grief, overwhelming grief, after the first intense outbursts, one always feels like sleep. Condemned men always sleep very soundly on their last night, so they say. That's how it should be, it's the way of nature, otherwise one couldn't stand the strain ... I lay down on the sofa, but didn't fall asleep ...

... During the six weeks of her illness, we tended her day and night—I, Lukeriya, and a qualified nurse from the hospital, whom I had hired. I didn't grudge the money, I positively felt like spending for her sake. I called in Doctor Schroeder and paid him ten roubles a visit. When she had recovered consciousness, I began keeping out of her sight. Why mention that, though? When she was up and about, she would quietly sit in my room, saying nothing, at a special table I had also bought for her ... Yes, it's true, we never exchanged a word; I mean we did start after a while, but it was always just the usual things. Of course, I deliberately refrained from broadening the conversation, but I became keenly conscious that she too was glad not to say anything beyond what was strictly necessary. I regarded that as perfectly natural on her part: 'She's too shaken and crushed', I thought, 'and of course she needs time to forget and get used to things.' So it was that we remained silent about it, but at every moment I was preparing myself for the future. I imagined she was doing the same, and I found it terribly exciting to guess: what exactly is she thinking now?

One more thing: oh, of course, no one can know how much I suffered, as I sighed over her during her illness. But my groans were inward, and I kept them suppressed deep within, even from Lukeriya. I could not imagine, not even envisage that she might die without learning everything. When she was out of danger and her health began to return, I recall that my peace of mind came back swiftly and in full measure. Moreover, I resolved to *postpone our future* for as long a time as possible, and leave everything meanwhile in the present tense. Yes, something strange and peculiar had happened to me, there is no other way I can describe it: I had triumphed, and the mere awareness of the fact was enough for me. Thus passed the entire winter. Ah, I had never been as contented as I was then, and for a whole winter at that.

In my life, do you see, there was one terrible external circumstance which, right up to the calamity with my wife, weighed upon me every hour of every day—namely my loss of reputation and departure from the regiment. Put briefly, it had been a despotic injustice perpetrated against me. True, my difficult, perhaps even absurd character told against me with my comrades, although it does often happen, doesn't it, that something you privately reverence and regard as exalted can seem at the same time unaccountably funny to the bulk of those about you? Oh, I was never popular, even at school. I was never popular anywhere. Even Lukeriya cannot feel a fondness towards me. Although the regimental incident was a result of dislike towards me, it was nevertheless fortuitous. I would add that there is nothing more exasperating and intolerable than to be undone by some chance incident which might just as easily not have occurred, as a result of some random aggregation of circumstances, which might have passed by like a cloud. For a creature of intelligence, it is humiliating. The incident was as follows.

During a theatre interval I had gone out to the bar. A hussar, A——v, suddenly entered and, in front of the officers and public present, struck up a loud conversation with two of his fellow hussars to the effect that Captain Bezumtsev of our regiment had just created a scene in the corridor and was 'apparently drunk'. The conversation petered out and was in any case misinformed, because Captain Bezumtsev wasn't drunk and the scene was actually nothing of the sort. The hussars changed the subject and there the matter ended, but the following day the story reached our regiment and it immediately began to be put about that I had been the only officer of the regiment in the bar and when the hussar A——v had insolently referred to Captain Bezumtsev I had not gone up to him and cut him short with a reproof. But why should I? If he had some sort of grudge against Bezumtsev, that was their private affair—why should I get involved? And yet the officers began to regard it as touching the regiment as well, and since I had been the only one of our officers present, I had demonstrated to all the officers and members of the public in the bar that there might be officers in our regiment who were not too exercised concerning their own honour and that of their regiment. I could not assent to this interpretation. I was informed that I could still rectify matters even now, if rather belatedly, by formally settling the matter with A——v. I had no desire to do this and, since I was in an ill humour, haughtily declined. Immediately after that I tendered my resignation—end of story. I left with pride, but my spirit was broken. My will and intellect sank into depression. Just at this juncture it so happened that my brother-in-law in Moscow dissipated our meagre resources, my own among them—a tiny portion of the whole, to be sure, but I was left out on the street without a kopek. I might have taken civil employment, but did not do so: after that splendid uniform I just couldn't go off and work on the railway somewhere. And so, shame if it must be, disgrace if it must be, degradation too, and the worse it was, the better—that was what I chose.

   Three years of grim memories followed, even the Vyazemsky House. Eighteen months ago, my rich old godmother died in Moscow, unexpectedly leaving me, among others, three thousand in her will. After some deliberation I decided upon my future there and then. I made up my mind to go into pawnbroking, without anyone else's by-your-leave: money, then a place to live and—a new life far from any former memories; that was the plan. Nevertheless, the dark shadow of the past and the permanent stain on my reputation tormented me every hour, every minute. But then I married. Coincidence or not, I don't know. In taking her into my house I thought it was as a friend, I really did have sore need of a friend. But I could see very well that such a friend had to be prepared, moulded, overmastered even. Could I really have explained anything just like that to this 16-year-old, full of prejudices as she was? For example, how could I have convinced her, without the chance assistance of the grim calamity of the revolver, that I wasn't a coward, and that the regiment had unjustly accused me? That calamity had occurred just at the right time. In withstanding the revolver, I had avenged all my grim past history. And although no one knew of it, *she* did, and that was all that mattered to me, because she herself was all in all to me, the sum of my future hopes and dreams! She was the sole person that I was making ready for me, there was no need of anyone else—and now she had realized everything; she had learned at least that she had behaved unjustly in so hastily allying herself with my enemies. This thought enraptured me. I could no longer be a blackguard in her eyes, at most a rather odd individual, but even that notion, after all that had passed, was by no means displeasing to me: oddity is not a vice, on the contrary it is sometimes found appealing by the female character. In short, I deliberately postponed the denouement; what had occurred was, for the moment, more than enough for my peace of mind and contained more than enough in the way of scenes and other material for my dreams. That's the wretched thing about it, I'm a dreamer: I had enough material, and as regards her, in my view *she could wait*.

So a whole winter went by, in the vague expectation of something happening. I took pleasure in glancing furtively at her, when she chanced to be sitting at her little table. She busied herself with sewing and occasionally read works she got from my bookcase. The range of books there should also weigh in my favour. She hardly ever went out. Every day, after dinner, before it got dark, I would take her out for a walk, and we took our exercise, but not in total silence as before. I actually did try to pretend that we were not avoiding any topic and were conversing in friendly fashion, but as I have already said, both of us made sure the talk was restricted. I was doing this deliberately, in order to 'give her time'. It was odd, of course, that it never once occurred to me until almost the end of winter that here I was enjoying watching her surreptitiously, and I hadn't caught a single glance of hers in my direction the whole time! I regarded that as diffidence on her part. Besides which, she had such an air of timid submission and weakness after her illness. No, best to wait it out and 'she'll come to you of her own accord . . .'.

This thought gave me irresistible pleasure. I would add one thing: sometimes I seemed to rouse myself deliberately, screwing my spirit and mind up to the point where I could nurture a resentment towards her. So matters proceeded for some time. But my hatred could never ripen and take firm root in my soul. Besides, I could sense myself that this was really all a game. Even then, although I had disrupted the marriage by purchasing the bed and screens, I could never, ever look upon her as a criminal. And not because I took a casual view of her transgression. It was because I intended to forgive her absolutely, from the very first day, even before I bought the bed. Actually, that was odd behaviour on my part because I am morally unbending. On the other hand, I saw her as being so defeated and humiliated, so crushed, that I sometimes felt agonizingly sorry for her, though at the same time I did occasionally relish the thought of her humiliation. The notion of the inequality between us was an appealing one . . .

I deliberately carried out a number of good deeds that winter. I let two people off what they owed, I gave money to one poor woman without a pledge. And I didn't tell my wife about that, I didn't do it hoping she would find out either; however, the woman herself came to thank me, practically on her knees. So in this way word got around; I received the impression that she really was pleased when she heard about the woman.

But spring was coming on, we were half-way through April by now, the double window-frames had been removed and the sun began to illumine our silent rooms with its bright beams. But scales hung before me and obscured my mind. Fateful, terrible scales! How did it come about that all this fell from my eyes, that all of a sudden I saw the light and understood everything? Was it by chance, or did some appointed day arrive, or did a sunbeam kindle thought and perception in my dulled mind? No, there was no thought or perception involved, it was a nerve that suddenly began to twitch; long numbed, it now began to quiver, and revived to light up the whole of my sluggard soul and my satanic pride. It was as if I had suddenly leapt up from my chair. And it happened abruptly, completely out of the blue. It happened towards evening, at about five o'clock in the afternoon.

II. The Scales Suddenly Fell

A WORD or two before I start. For a month I had marked in her a strange pensiveness, not silence exactly, I mean pensiveness. This was also something I noticed suddenly. She was seated at her work, inclining her head over her sewing, unaware that I was looking at her. Then all at once it struck me how slender she'd grown, thin, her face so pale, her lips ashen—all this, taken together with her pensive air, came as a severe and sudden shock. I had already noticed her dry little cough previously, during the night especially. I stood up at once and, without telling her, set off to ask Doctor Schroeder to call.

Schroeder arrived the following day. She was most taken aback and looked from one to another of us.

'Oh, I'm healthy enough', she said, with a vague smile. Schroeder didn't examine her very thoroughly (these doctors can often be patronizingly negligent) and only told me in the other room, that it was the after-effects of her illness and it would be no bad thing when spring arrived to take her off somewhere to the seaside or, if that was out of the question, to a cottage in the country; in effect, he told me nothing except that there was a weakness or something of that nature. When Schroeder had gone, she suddenly told me again, staring at me with the utmost gravity:

'I am quite, quite well.'

But saying this she flushed all of a sudden, evidently out of embarrassment. Obviously that was it. Oh, now I understand: she felt embarrassed that I was still her *husband*, concerned about her, as if I were a genuine husband. But at the time, I didn't realize this and put it down to her meekness. (Scales!)

And so, a month later in April, at getting on for five on a bright, sunny day, I was sitting in the office doing my accounts. Then all at once I heard her, as she worked at her table in our room, ever so quietly . . . start singing. This new phenomenon produced a stunning effect on me, indeed I don't understand it to this day. Up till then I had practically never heard her sing, except in the very first days, when I brought her home and we could still indulge in high spirits, firing at the target. At that time, her voice had been quite strong and resonant, a bit uncertain, but wonderfully pleasant and powerful. Now, however, the song was so faint—I don't mean mournful (it was a romance of some sort) but it was as if there was something cracked, or broken, as if the little voice could not cope, as if the song itself were ill. She was singing under her breath and, as it rose, suddenly the voice broke off—such a forlorn little voice, and it broke off so piteously she cleared her throat and again, ever so quietly, resumed her faint singing . . .

Some may laugh at my emotion, but no one will ever understand why I was so agitated! No, I wasn't sorry for her as yet, this was something of a different order altogether. I felt a kind of sudden bewilderment, at least in those first moments, a terrible surprise, terrible and strange, morbid and almost vengeful: 'Singing, and in my presence! *Can she have forgotten about me?*'

Thoroughly dismayed, I remained where I was, then abruptly got up, got my hat, and went out, my mind a blank. Certainly I had no notion of where I was going or why. Lukeriya helped me on with my coat.

'She sings?' I couldn't help asking her. She didn't take this in and stared at me uncomprehendingly; I actually was incoherent at that.

'Is this the first time she's been singing?'

'No, she sometimes sings when you're not here,' Lukeriya replied.

It all comes back to me. I descended the staircase, went out into the street, and set off blindly. I got as far as the corner and started staring into space. People went past, jostling me as I stood oblivious. I hailed a cabby and directed him to the Politseisky Bridge,* for some reason. But I suddenly abandoned that idea and gave him twenty kopeks:

'That's for your trouble', I said, with a fatuous laugh, but a kind of rapture had begun to well up in my heart.

I turned for home, increasing my pace. The cracked, forlorn, interrupted note again suddenly echoed through my soul. I caught my breath. The scales were falling, falling from my eyes! If she could sing in my presence, that meant that she had forgotten about me—that fact was clear and terrible. My heart sensed it. But the rapture shone forth in my soul and overcame the fear.

Ah, the irony of fate! There might have been, could have been nothing else in my soul all winter but that same rapture, but where had I been all winter? Had my soul and I been together at all? I ran up the stairs in a flurry, I don't know if my entrance was shamefaced or not. All I remember is that the whole floor seemed to be undulating and I afloat on a river. I went in; she was sitting in her former place, sewing with head bent, but no longer singing. She gave me a fleeting incurious glance, but it wasn't really a glance—only a gesture, routine and indifferent, as when someone enters a room.

I went straight to her and sat down near her chair, like a madman. She looked swiftly at me, apparently alarmed: I took her arm and I don't remember what I said to her, I mean intended to say, because I couldn't even talk properly. My voice refused to obey me and kept breaking off. I didn't know what to say either, I just kept gasping.

'Let's talk . . . you know . . . say something!' I blurted out something stupid. Oh, did it matter if I made sense? She gave another start and recoiled in considerable alarm as she stared at my face, but all of a sudden her eyes expressed *cool astonishment*. Yes, astonishment, and *cool* at that. She stared at me, wide-eyed. This coolness, this cool surprise shattered me: 'So you still want love? Love?' was the question that surprise seemed to ask, though she remained mute. But I read it all, everything. My whole being shook as I collapsed at her feet. Yes, I fell down at her feet. She quickly got up, but I restrained her, gripping both her arms with considerable force.

And I was realizing my despair to the full, ah, indeed I was! But if you can believe it, such wild rapture was seething in my heart that I thought I should die. I kissed her feet in ecstasy and happiness. Yes, happiness, boundless and measureless, and all this in full realization of my hopeless despair. I wept, tried to say something and couldn't. Her alarm and astonishment gave place to preoccupation with some idea, some question of vast import, and she looked at me strangely, wildly even, she urgently wanted to comprehend something of this and smiled. She was terribly embarrassed at my kissing her feet and withdrew them, but I immediately set about kissing the spot on the floor where they had rested. She saw this and suddenly started laughing from sheer embarrassment (you know how people laugh out of embarrassment). Hysteria wasn't far away, I could see; her hands were shaking—I ignored that and kept on muttering that I loved her, that I wouldn't get up, 'let me kiss your dress . . . pray to you all my life like this . . .' I don't know, don't remember—then she burst out into sobs and started shaking; a terrible fit of hysteria had set in. I had frightened her.

I carried her over to the bed. When the fit had passed, she sat up and with a ghastly dazed expression on her face, seized my hands and implored me to calm myself: 'That's enough now, don't torment yourself, calm down!' and commenced weeping again. All that evening I never left her side. I kept telling her that I would take her away to Boulogne to bathe in the sea, now, this minute, in a fortnight's time, that she had such a cracked little voice, I'd heard it not long back, that I'd close the business and sell it to Dobronravov, that everything would start anew, but the main thing was Boulogne, Boulogne! She listened but her fear was unabated. Indeed her fear grew and grew. But this mattered less to me than my overwhelming desire to lie at her feet and kiss the floor again, kiss where her feet were resting, and pray to her and—'I will ask nothing more of you, nothing', I kept repeating. 'Don't answer me, ignore me altogether, just let me look at you from a corner, regard me as your chattel, your lapdog . . .' She was crying.

'*But I thought you were going to leave me like that*', all at once came blurting out involuntarily, so much so that she may not have noticed what she had said at all, and yet—ah, that was the most important, most fateful thing she had said that evening, and the most explicit; it slashed me like a knife across the heart! It explained everything to me, everything, but while she was close to me, before my eyes, I went on wildly hoping and was happy. Ah, I wearied her terribly that evening; I knew that, but kept on thinking that I might bring about some sudden alteration. Eventually, towards nightfall, she became utterly exhausted and I persuaded her to sleep. She dropped off soundly at once. I expected delirium and and it did come, but only very slightly. I got up constantly through the night and came in quietly in my slippers to look at her. I wrung my hands over her, looking at the sick creature on that wretched cot, the iron bedstead I had bought her for three roubles. I would kneel down but did not venture to kiss her feet as she slept (without her leave!). I would kneel to pray, and then leap to my feet again. Lukeriya emerged from the kitchen now and again to keep a close eye on me. I went and told her to lie down and that tomorrow something 'quite different' would commence.

And I believed that—blindly, insanely, horribly. Oh, the bliss, the bliss that flooded through me! I couldn't wait for the morrow. Above all, I couldn't believe that anything at all could go wrong, in spite of the warning signs. My reasoning powers had still not wholly returned, fallen scales notwithstanding; nor did they for long enough—until today, in fact, until this very day! Anyway, how could they have come back to me then, how could they: she was still alive then, wasn't she, she was here right in front of me, as I was before her. 'She'll wake up tomorrow and I'll tell her everything and she will see it all.' That was my reasoning at the time, simple and clear, hence my blissful feelings! Above all, there was this trip to Boulogne. I kept thinking that Boulogne was everything, that Boulogne held the final key to it all. 'To Boulogne, to Boulogne! . . .' I awaited the morning in a state of frenzy.

III. I Understand Only too Well

AND that was just a few days ago, you know, five days, only five days—last Tuesday! No, no, if I'd had just a little more time, if she'd just waited a tiny bit longer I would have dispelled the darkness! And she had calmed down, hadn't she? The very next day she was listening to me with a smile, despite her bewilderment . . . The main point was that all that time, all the five days, she was a prey to bewilderment or embarrassment. She was afraid too, very much so. I won't argue, I won't be mad enough to deny it: there was fear, but it was perfectly understandable. After all, we had been alien to one another for so long, grown apart so far, then all at once, this . . . But I paid no attention to her fears, a new sun was shining!

It's true, indubitably true, that I committed an error. Perhaps a good many errors. As soon as we awoke the next day, first thing in the morning (this was on the Wednesday) I at once made a mistake: I immediately started treating her as a friend. I was in a hurry, far too much of a hurry, but I had to confess, more than confess, it was a driving necessity. I did not even dissemble what I had concealed from myself all my life. I told her plainly that for the whole of that winter the one thing I had been certain of was her love. I explained that the pawnbroking business had been merely the low ebb of my will and reason, a private notion of self-flagellation and self-glorification. I explained to her that I really had exhibited cowardice back then in the bar, that this reflected my character and mistrustful nature: I'd been overwhelmed by the situation, the bar, the thought of how to get out of it without appearing ridiculous. I wasn't afraid of a duel, but of fearing to seem ridiculous . . . Afterwards I had not wanted to admit all this, and had made everybody, including her, miserable on that account, and had even married her to make her life a misery because of it. Altogether I talked for the most part as if I were feverish. She herself took me by the hand and begged me to stop: 'You're exaggerating . . . you're torturing yourself.' The tears would start again, bordering on hysteria! She kept begging me not to tell her of any of this, not keep bringing it back to mind.

I ignored these pleas or paid them little heed: spring, Boulogne! There was the sun, our new sun, I talked of nothing else. I closed down the shop and handed the business over to Dobronravov. I suggested to her that we distribute everything to the poor, apart from the original three thousand which my godmother had given me and which would finance the trip to Boulogne, after which we would return and start out on a new working life. So it was resolved, because she didn't say a word . . . just smiled. Probably a tactful smile, so as not to upset me. I could see of course that I was a burden to her, don't think I was such a selfish fool as not to see that. I saw it all, right down to the last detail, I saw and realized better than anyone; the extent of my desperation was obvious to anyone!

I talked to her about myself and about her too. And about Lukeriya. I talked about my weeping . . . And I did change the subject too, I also tried to keep off certain topics at all costs. And she did grow positively animated on one or two occasions, I remember, I do remember that! Why do you say that I looked and saw nothing? And if only *that* had not happened, everything would have come alive again. Wasn't she telling me only the day before yesterday, when the talk got on to books and what she'd read that winter, she was telling me about them and laughing at the recollection of the scene between Gil Blas and the Archbishop of Grenada.* And such sweet, childlike laughter it was, just like before we were married (an instant! A fleeting instant!); how glad I was! I was amazed, incidentally, by this about the Archbishop: after all, she must have recovered a great deal of peace of mind if she could laugh over a masterpiece as she sat there that winter. She must have begun to recover her equilibrium altogether, begun to be wholly convinced that I would leave her *like that*. 'I thought you were going to leave me *like that*',

that was what she had come out with that Tuesday, wasn't it? Ah, the thinking of a 10-year-old girl! And she had believed, really believed, that things would actually remain *like that*: she at her table, I at mine, and so it would be till 60. Then suddenly—I come forward, a husband, and a husband needs love! Oh, the misunderstanding, my utter blindness!

Another mistake was in looking at her so rapturously; it frightened her; I should have held back. But I was holding back, wasn't I? I'd stopped kissing her feet. I never once made a show of being . . . well, a husband—oh, that never entered my head either, I simply prayed! But after all, I couldn't just say nothing at all! I told her abruptly that I enjoyed her conversation, and that I regarded her as incomparably, incomparably more cultured and mature than I was. She got flustered and went very red, saying that I was exaggerating. At which point, fool that I was, I couldn't refrain from saying how thrilled I had been behind the door to hear her duel, that duel of innocence with that creature; how I had enjoyed her cleverness, her flashing wit coupled with her childlike simplicity of manner. She seemed to give a start, and began prattling again that I was exaggerating, but all at once, her face darkened as she buried it in her hands and began to sob . . . At this point I just couldn't hold out: I fell before her again, and began kissing her feet once more, the upshot being another hysterical fit, the same as happened on Tuesday. That was yesterday evening, and next morning . . .

Next morning?! Have I gone mad? Next morning was this morning, a while ago, just a while ago!

Listen and try to grasp what I am saying: when we met a while ago by the samovar (after yesterday's fit) I was astonished at how collected she was—and she really was, you know! As for me, I'd spent all night shaking with fear over what had happened that day. But all at once she came over and stood facing me with folded arms (this morning, just a while ago!) and began to tell me that she knew she was a criminal, and that her crime had been tormenting her all winter and did so now . . . she appreciated my generosity greatly . . . 'I will be your faithful wife, I will respect you . . .'

At this, I leapt to my feet and like a madman embraced her. I kissed her, kissed her face, her lips, like a husband does his wife after a long separation. Why did I have to go out this morning, even just for two hours . . . our passports . . . Oh God! If I'd only got back five minutes, five minutes sooner! . . . There was that crowd outside our gate, the looks they gave me . . . Lord in heaven!

Lukeriya says (oh, I'm not letting Lukeriya go for anything now, she knows it all, she was here the whole winter, she'll tell me all about it), she says that after I had left the house and some twenty minutes before my return, she had suddenly gone in to her mistress in our room to ask something, I've forgotten what, and saw that she had taken out her icon (that same icon of the Madonna) and it was standing before her on the table. It looked as if she had just been praying to it. 'What's the matter, mistress?' 'It's all right, Lukeriya, you may go . . . Wait, Lukeriya', she went up to her and kissed her. 'Are you happy, mistress?' 'Yes, Lukeriya.' 'It was high time the master came and begged forgiveness . . . The Lord be thanked that you have made your peace together.' 'All right, Lukeriya, you may go', she smiled, you know, in a funny way. So strangely, that ten minutes later Lukeriya came back suddenly to keep an eye on her: 'She was standing by the wall, right by the window, with one arm resting against the wall, and her head pressed against it, just standing there thinking. So preoccupied was she, that she didn't hear me standing watching her from the other room. I saw she was sort of smiling, standing there, thinking and smiling. I watched her, then turned and went out quietly, wondering to myself. Then I suddenly heard a window being opened. I went in at once to say: 'It's chilly out, mistress, be sure you don't catch cold', then the next thing I see, she's got up on the sill and is standing bolt upright in the open window, with her back to me, holding the icon in her hands. My heart sank. I shouted: 'Mistress, mistress!' She heard me and moved as if to turn round, but instead, stepped forward, clutching the icon to her breast, and hurled herself from the window!'

All I remember is that when I came in through the gate, she was still warm. And chiefly, that they were all staring at me. At first there was shouting, then a sudden silence as everyone fell back and she . . . she lay with the icon. I recall, as if through a blanket of dark, going up to her in silence and staring at her for a long time, and everyone crowding round and saying things. Lukeriya was there too, but I didn't see her. She says she spoke to me. I only recall that tradesman: he kept shouting at me that 'a handful of blood came out of her mouth, a handful, a handful!' and pointing to the blood there on the stone. I think I touched the blood with my finger, staining it, looking at the finger (that I remember) while he kept on at me about 'a handful, a handful!'

'What do you mean, a handful?' I yelled at the top of my voice and flung myself at him, so they say . . .

Oh, monstrous, monstrous! The misunderstanding! How could it be! It's impossible!

IV. Just Five Minutes too Late

ISN'T that right? Was it in the realms of probability? It can't be said to be possible, can it? Why, for what reason did that woman die?

Oh, believe me, I understand; but the reason she died is still an open question. She was afraid of my love and asked herself seriously whether she should accept it or not, could not bear the dilemma, and found it better to die. I know, I know, it's plain enough; she had made too many promises and got frightened that she couldn't keep them—it's obvious. There are some truly horrible considerations involved.

Because for what reason did she die? The question won't go away. That question throbs and throbs within my brain. I would have left her *like that* if she had wanted things to stay *like that*. She didn't believe it, that was the trouble! No, no, I'm not telling the truth, it's not that at all. It's just that with me she had to be honest: love wholeheartedly if love at all, not the way she would have loved the trader. And since she was too chaste, too pure to assent to the love the trader would have wanted, she didn't want to deceive me either. She had no desire to deceive me with half-love masquerading as the real thing, or quarter-love. Too honest, that's what! I wanted to inject a breadth of understanding back then, remember? Strange notion.

I'm terribly curious about one thing: did she respect me? I don't know if she despised me or not. It's terribly odd: why did it never once enter my head all winter that she might hold me in contempt? I had been firmly convinced of the opposite, right up to the moment when she had looked at me in *cool astonishment*. There and then I realized that she despised me. Realized irrevocably, for ever. Ah well, suppose she did despise me, what if she despised me all her life—if only she were alive, alive now! Just a little while ago she was walking about and talking. I utterly fail to understand why she flung herself from the window! And how could I have imagined such a thing five minutes beforehand? I've called Lukeriya. I shan't let Lukeriya go now, not for anything, not for anything!

Oh, we could still have come to an agreement. It was just that we had grown terribly far apart during the winter, but surely we could have got used to one another again? Why, why couldn't we have come together and begun a new life again? I am generous-hearted and so is she—there's the point of contact! Just a few more words, two days, no more than that, and she would have understood everything.

. The main thing that outrages me is that it was all by chance—plain, brute, blind chance. That's the exasperating thing! Five minutes, that's all, just five minutes and the moment would have passed by like a cloud, and it would never have entered her head again. And the end result would have been total comprehension on her part. But now it's back to empty rooms, and I am alone again. There's the pendulum ticking away, it's all one to that, it's not sorry for anyone. There's no one, that's the awful thing!

I am pacing the room, I keep on doing that. I know, I know, no prompting please; you find it absurd that I'm railing against chance and a matter of five minutes? But there's an obvious point here. Bear one thing in mind; she didn't even leave a note behind, along the lines of: 'No one's to blame for my death', the way everybody does. Surely she must have realized that she might even land Lukeriya in trouble: 'She was alone with her', people might have said, 'So she was the one who pushed her.' Had it not been for four people who had seen her from the windows of the adjoining wing and the courtyard, standing there with the icon and flinging herself down, they might well have taken Lukeriya away, innocent as she was. But this too was mere chance, wasn't it, that people were standing and saw what happened? No, all this—was a matter of an instant, just one inexplicable instant. Something sudden, a fleeting whim! What does it matter if she was praying to the icon? That doesn't mean she was contemplating death. The whole business lasted a matter of ten minutes or so, the whole decision took place precisely at the time when she was standing by the wall, leaning her head against her arm and smiling. The notion flashed into her head, started spinning round, and she couldn't hold out against it.

It was a plain misunderstanding, say what you like. She could have gone on living with me. And what about anaemia? Just simple anaemia, from the exhaustion of her vital energies? She'd got worn out over the winter, that was the way of it . . .

I was too late!!!

How thin she is in the coffin, how sharp her little nose has got. Her eyelashes are like needles. And the way she fell, you know, nothing shattered, nothing broken. Just a 'handful of blood'. Meaning a dessert-spoonful. Internal injuries. A strange thought: what if I don't have to bury her? Because if they take her away . . . oh no, it's practically unthinkable that they should do that! Oh, I know they have to take her away, I haven't lost my mind and I'm not raving in the slightest, on the contrary my brain has never been so lucid—but how can I carry on with no one in the house again, two rooms again, on my own again among the pledges? Raving! That's where the raving comes in! I wore her out—that's what!

What are your laws to me now? What is the point of your customs, mores, your state or your religion? Let your judges sit in judgement upon me, let me be brought to court, open court, and I will say that I recognize nothing. The judge will shout: 'Be quiet, officer!' And I will shout back: 'What power do you have now to make me obey? Why has grim inertia smashed what was most dear to me? What are your laws to me now? I part company with them.' Oh, what do I care!

Blind, blind! Dead and cannot hear me! You cannot know the paradise I would have girded about you. That paradise was in my soul, I would have planted it around you! Well, you wouldn't have loved me—so be it, what does it matter. Everything would have been *like that*, everything would have stayed *like that*. You would have told me about it as a friend— we would have rejoiced and laughed happily, looking one another in the eye. That's how we would have lived. And if you took a fancy to someone else—well all right, all right! You would walk with him, laughing, and I would watch from the other side of the street . . . Oh anything would be all right if only she would open her eyes just once! For one instant, just one! To look at me the way she did this morning when she stood before me and vowed to be a faithful wife! Oh, in one glance she would understand everything!

Inertia . . . Oh, nature! People on earth are alone, that is the calamity of it! 'Is anyone alive on the plain?' shouts the old Russian hero, and no one responds. I am no epic hero, but I too shout, and no one responds. They say the sun animates the universe. The sun will rise and look at it—is it not a corpse? Everything is dead and corpses are everywhere. Only people exist and around them is silence—that is what the earth is! 'People, love one another!'* Who said that? Whose behest is that? The pendulum ticks on, insensible, horrible. It's two o'clock in the morning. Her shoes are standing by her little bed, as if they expected her . . . no, seriously, when they take her away tomorrow, what on earth am I going to do?

THE DREAM OF A
RIDICULOUS MAN

THE DREAM OF A
RIDICULOUS MAN

A FANTASTIC STORY

I

I AM a ridiculous man. Nowadays they call me mad. That would be a step up in rank if they did not also persist in regarding me as ridiculous. But these days I no longer get angry about that; these days they are all dear to my heart and even when they make fun of me, then too, for some reason, I cherish them—if anything, even more. I would join in the laughter—not so much at myself, but out of love for them— if it didn't make me so sad to look upon them. Sad, because they do not know the truth, whereas I do. Ah, how painful it is to be the only one to know the truth! But they won't understand this. No, they won't understand.

Formerly, I used to anguish a great deal over the fact that I seemed odd. Was, not seemed. I was always peculiar, and I have been aware of this from the day I was born. Perhaps as early as 7 years old I was aware of my oddity. After that I went to school, then the university, and what do you think— the more I studied, the more it was borne in upon me that I was odd. For me, therefore, it was as if the sole point of my entire university course had ultimately been to demonstrate and make clear to me how peculiar I was. As in my studies, so in life. With each passing year, this same awareness of the ridiculous figure I cut in all respects grew and strengthened. I was laughed at by everyone upon every occasion. But no one knew or guessed that if there was a man on this earth who knew better than anyone how ridiculous I was, that man was myself, and that was the thing I found most exasperating of all, that they did not know it. It was my own fault, however: I was always so proud that I wouldn't have wanted to admit it for the world. This pride grew within me as time went by, and if I had ever chanced to allow myself to admit I was ridiculous to anyone at all, then I think I would have blown my head off with a revolver then and there, that very evening. Ah, how I suffered in my adolescence over whether I might break down and blurt it out unprompted to my schoolfellows. But since I came of age, although with every year that passes I have learned more and more about this frightful quality of mine, I have unaccountably grown somewhat calmer. I use the word 'unaccountably' because up to now I have failed to determine why this should be so. Perhaps it was because a terrible anguish had developed within my soul, occasioned by a circumstance which loomed infinitely larger than my own self: to be precise, it was the dawning conviction that in the world at large, *nothing mattered*. I had had a presentiment of this for a good long time, but complete conviction came swiftly during this last year. All of a sudden, I realized that it *would not matter* to me whether the world existed or whether there was nothing at all anywhere. I began to intuit and sense with all my being, that *there was nothing around me*. At first I was inclined to think that in the past there had been a great deal, but later on I divined that formerly too there had been nothing, it had merely seemed otherwise for some reason. I gradually became convinced that there would be nothing in the future either. It was then that I suddenly stopped being angry at other people and almost ceased to notice them. Indeed this became apparent even in the most trivial matters: for example, I would bump into people as I was walking along the street. Not because I was preoccupied either: what had I got to be preoccupied about? I'd given up thinking altogether at that point: it was all one to me. And it would have been all right if I had been resolving problems—alas, not a one did I solve, and how many there were! But I had grown *indifferent* and the questions faded into the background.

So then, it was subsequent to all this that I learned the truth. I learned the truth last November, the 3rd of the month to be precise, and since then I can recall my every moment. It happened on a dismal evening, the most dismal there could possibly be. I was returning home some time after eleven, and I remember I was actually reflecting that there could not possibly be a more dismal hour. Even in a physical sense. Rain had poured down all day, rain of the coldest and most cheerless kind, a sort of menacing rain, I remember, openly hostile towards human beings. And now, after ten, it abruptly ceased, to be replaced by a fearful dankness, colder and damper than when the rain had been falling. Everything seemed to give off a kind of steam, every cobble in the street, every alleyway, if one peered deep down into it from the street. I suddenly pictured to myself that if the gaslights were to be extinguished everywhere things would be more cheerful, because gaslight saddened the heart by illuminating all this. I had barely had anything for dinner that day and from early evening I had been at a certain engineer's; there were two other friends there too. I had said little and I think they found that trying. They were talking about some provocative topic and all of a sudden grew positively heated. But they didn't care, I could see that, and they were getting worked up just for the sake of it. I abruptly came out with: 'Gentlemen, you know you don't care, do you?' They took no offence and there was general laughter at my expense. This was because I had spoken without reproof and it had meant nothing to me. They saw my indifference and this tickled them.

While I was thinking about the gaslight in the street, I glanced upward at the sky. It was horribly dark, and yet I could clearly make out ragged clouds and, between them, fathomless black spaces. Suddenly, I noticed in one of these spaces a tiny star and began watching it intently. That was because that tiny star had given me an idea: I decided to kill myself that night. I had firmly resolved on this two months before, in fact, and in spite of my poverty had purchased a handsome revolver and loaded it that very day. Two months had already passed, however, and it was still lying in the drawer; but at the time I had felt so utterly apathetic, that in the end it had seemed preferable to choose a moment when it would mean more to me—why, I don't know. Thus, for the last two months, every night as I was returning home, I was thinking I would shoot myself. I was just waiting for the moment. And now this star had given me an idea, and I resolved that it would be *this night* without fail. But why the star had put the idea into my head, I don't know.

So it happened, that while I was gazing up at the sky, this little girl seized my elbow. The street was deserted by now, and there was practically nobody about. In the distance, a cabby was asleep in his droshky.* The little girl was about 8 years old, and all she had on was a wretched little dress and a kerchief on her head; she was wet through, but I took special note of her tattered wet shoes; I remember them still, they were what particularly caught my eye. She suddenly started tugging at my elbow and calling to me. She wasn't crying, but kept jerking out some words, which she couldn't articulate properly because she was all a-tremble and shivering with cold. For some reason she was terrified and kept shouting desperately: 'Mummy! Mummy!' I turned to face her, but said not a word and went on walking along; but she kept running and tugging at me, and her voice held that sound indicative of desperation in children who are very frightened. I know that sound. Although she had not managed to get a word out properly, I realized that her mother was dying somewhere, or something had happened to them and she had run out to call someone or find something to help her mother. But I didn't follow her; on the contrary, it suddenly occurred to me to chase her away. At first I told her to go and look for a policeman, but she just folded her little arms and kept running alongside, sobbing and out of breath, and would not leave me. At that I stamped my foot at her and shouted. She merely cried out: Sir, sir! . . .', but all at once abandoned me and raced headlong across the street: another passer-by had hove into view and she had evidently rushed off to him.

I ascended to my fourth floor. I rent one of the rooms in the house. My room is small and mean, with a semi-circular attic window. I have an oilcloth sofa, a table with my books on it, two chairs, and an armchair—Voltaire-style, though ancient as can be. I sat down, lit a candle, and fell to thinking. In the room next door, the bedlam was continuing. It had been going on since the day before yesterday. A retired captain lived there and he had visitors, some six civilians;

they were drinking vodka and playing shtos* with old cards. There had been a free fight the previous night, and I know for a fact that two of them dragged one another round by the hair for quite a time. The landlady would like to complain but she's terrified of the captain. We only have one other tenant, a small, slender lady, a newly arrived army wife, with three small children who have already fallen ill here in our lodging-house. Both she and the children are mortally afraid of the captain and shudder and cross themselves all night; the smallest child has been terrified into some sort of seizure. I know for a fact that this captain occasionally stops passers-by on Nevsky Prospect and begs money from them. Nobody will give him a job, but oddly enough (and this is the point I'm getting at), over the whole month he has been living here, the captain has not caused me the least annoyance. I declined his acquaintance of course from the very first, and he found me a bore from the outset too, but however much they might shout behind their partition, and however many of them there might be—it never bothers me. I sit there all night and really I never hear them, so oblivious am I. I never go to sleep till dawn anyway—and that's been going on for a year. I sit up through the night in the armchair by the table, doing nothing at all. I only read books during the day. I sit there without even thinking, just, you know, toying with various notions as I let them off the leash. The candle burns right down overnight.

I sat down at the table, retrieved the revolver, and placed it before me. When I had put it down, I remember asking myself: 'Right?' and replying quite positively: 'Right.' That is, I would shoot myself. I knew that I would certainly shoot myself that night, but how long I would go on sitting at the table, that I did not know. And I would indeed have shot myself of course, had it not been for that little girl.

II

So you see: although really I was indifferent, I did feel actual pain. If someone had struck me, I would have experienced pain. It was exactly the same in the moral sense: let something supremely pitiful occur, and I would feel pity, just as I had when I had not been indifferent to everything in life. Indeed, I had felt pity only a little while ago: I would certainly have helped that child. Why, then, had I not done so? Because of a thought which had occurred to me at the time: when she was tugging and calling out to me, a certain question had crossed my mind and I had been unable to answer it. The question was an idle one, but I was angered because it followed that once I had resolved to do away with myself that night, then everything in the world must perforce be a matter of indifference—indeed, more so than ever before. Why then this sudden sense that I was not indifferent and that I felt pity for the girl? I recall that I did pity her very much—to the point of experiencing a strange aching feeling, utterly incredible in the situation I was in. Really, I can't convey that fleeting sensation any more satisfactorily, but it also persisted at home when I had sat down at the table and I was exasperated in a way I had not been for long enough. Argument succeeded argument. It seemed clear that if I were a man and not yet a zero, while I had not yet become that zero, then I was alive and consequently could suffer, become angry, and feel shame for my actions. Very well. But then if I should kill myself in two hours' time, say, what would the little girl be to me and what would shame and indeed anything in the world mean to me?* I am reducing myself to a cipher, an absolute zero. And can it be that awareness of my imminent *absolute* extinction and the consequence that nothing will exist has not had the slightest influence either on my feeling of pity for the little girl, or my shame at a mean-spirited action? After all, the reason I stamped my foot at the unfortunate child and brutally shouted at her was because I told myself: 'not only am I deaf to pity, but even if I commit some inhuman villainy, I can do that now, because in two hours' time, all will be extinguished.' Do you believe that's why I shouted? I am almost convinced now that it was so. It seemed evident that life and the world depended on me. One might go so far as to say that the world was created for me alone, as it were: I will shoot myself and the world will cease to exist, at least for me. Not to mention that perhaps nothing will exist for anyone after me, and the whole world, as soon as my consciousness is extinguished, will pass away like a phantom, as an attribute of my consciousness, and will abolish itself, since perhaps all this world and all these people—are but my own self. I remember, as I sat there debating, I turned all these novel questions, crowding in upon me one after the other, in another direction entirely, and devised something altogether new. For example, a strange notion suddenly occurred to me, that if I had formerly lived on the moon or on Mars, and had there perpetrated the most shameful and dishonourable action one could possibly imagine, and had been execrated and disgraced, in some fashion that can only be experienced and imagined in occasional dreams, or nightmares, and if, once finding myself back on earth, I were to preserve the awareness of what I had done on that other planet, and moreover knew that I would never go back there under any circumstances—then, looking up at the moon from the earth, would I be *indifferent* or not? Would I feel shame for that action or not? These questions were idle and irrelevant, since the revolver was already lying in front of me, and I knew with every fibre of my being that *it* would certainly take place, but they excited and infuriated me. Somehow I was now unable to die without having first resolved something. In a nutshell, that little girl had saved me; my questionings had postponed the bullet. Meanwhile, in the captain's room, things were also quieter: they had finished playing cards, and were settling down for the night, grumbling the while and lazily exchanging a last curse. At this point I abruptly dropped of to sleep in my chair at the table, something that had never happened to me before. I didn't notice it happening at all. Dreams, as we know, are extremely strange things:* some parts have a horrific clarity, a jeweller's

finish in the details, while other parts are skipped over without
any account of space and time. Dreams seem to be driven
according to one's desires, rather than reason, the heart, not
the brain, and yet what prodigies of complexity did my reason
sometimes perform when I dreamed! Absolutely inconceiv-
able things happen to it in dreams. My brother, for example,
died five years ago. Sometimes I see him in my dreams: he
takes a hand in my affairs, we get engrossed, and yet
throughout the entire length of the dream, I know and
remember that my brother is dead and buried. How on earth
can I fail to be surprised that, despite being dead, he is busy
at my side? Why does my reason permit all this without
demur? Still, enough of that. Let me proceed to my dream.
Yes, that was when I had that dream of mine, the 3rd of
November! They tease me nowadays because it was just a
dream, after all. But does it matter whether it was a dream or
not, if that dream revealed the Truth to me? For once you
have learned the truth and seen it, you know it really is the
truth, that there is and can be no other, whether you are
asleep or awake. Well, what if it was a dream, what if it was?
This life you cry up so much is what I wanted to extinguish
by suicide, whereas my dream, my dream—oh, it has revealed
to me a great, new, regenerated intensity of life!

Listen.

III

I SAID that I fell asleep without noticing, while apparently
still deliberating over the matters I mentioned. All of a
sudden, I dreamed that I picked up the revolver and, as I sat
there, aimed it straight at my heart—the heart, not the head;
I had actually planned beforehand to shoot myself in the
head, in the right temple to be precise. Aiming at my chest, I
paused for a second or two and my candle, table, and wall
abruptly began to shift and sway. I quickly fired.

Sometimes in dreams you fall from a height, you are
slashed or beaten, but you never feel pain, unless you actually

do knock yourself against the bed: then you do feel pain and it almost always wakes you up. So it was in my dream: I felt no pain, but it seemed that after my shot, everything inside me was convulsed and suddenly extinguished; it grew horribly black all around me. I seemed to be blind and dumb as I lay stretched out on my back on something hard. I could see nothing and was incapable of the least movement. People around were walking and shouting, the captain's bass, the landlady's screaming—then another abrupt interval and I was being borne along in a closed coffin. I could feel the coffin rocking and I considered the matter; suddenly, for the first time, the idea struck me that I was actually dead, quite dead, I knew this as an indubitable fact. I could not see or move, and yet I could feel and think. But I quickly fell in with the situation, and as usually happens in dreams, accepted the reality without protest.

Now they were burying me in the earth. Everyone went away and I was alone. I did not move. Whenever I had day-dreamed about being buried, I had always associated the grave solely with cold and damp. Now I did feel very cold, especially the tips of my toes, but beyond that, I felt nothing. I lay there and, oddly, anticipated nothing, accepting without argument that a dead man has no expectations. But it was damp. I don't know how much time elapsed—an hour, a day, many days. But then all of a sudden, a drop of water, seeping through the coffin-lid, fell on to my closed left eye. It was followed a minute later by another, then a minute later by a third, and so on and on at regular minute intervals. Profound indignation flared in my heart and I suddenly felt a physical pain there: 'It's my wound', I thought, 'the shot, there's a bullet there.' And the drops kept falling every minute, directly on to my closed eye. I abruptly appealed, not with my voice, as I could not move, but with my entire being, to the arbiter of all that was happening to me:

'Whoever thou art, if thou art and if there exists something more rational than what is taking place at present, then grant it may have sway here too. However, if thou art taking vengeance for my ill-advised suicide—with the demeaning absurdity of continued being—then know that no torture which may be applied to me will ever be comparable to the mute contempt I shall feel throughout my martyrdom, though it last a million years! . . .'

I made my appeal and fell silent. A profound silence lasted for almost a minute, and another drop of water fell, but I knew and trusted, with a boundless and unshakeable conviction, that things would certainly change soon . . . And all at once my grave opened wide. I mean I did not know whether it had been opened up or dug open, but I was caught up by some unknown, mysterious creature and we found ourselves out in space. I suddenly recovered my sight: it was the deep of night; never, never had there ever been such blackness! We drifted through space, by now far away from earth. I did not ask whatever was carrying me any questions, I waited and retained my pride. I assured myself that I was not afraid, and fairly fainted with rapture at the thought that I felt no fear. I don't recall how long we drifted, nor can I conceive it: everything took place the way it always does in dreams, when you skip over space, time, and the laws of being and reason, pausing only at points the heart feels like selecting. I remember suddenly catching sight of a little star in the darkness. 'Is that Sirius?' I asked, my restraint breaking down, as I had not intended to ask any questions. 'No, it is the same star you saw between the clouds as you were returning home', responded the creature which had borne me away. I knew that it had a kind of human face. In a strange way, I didn't like the creature, indeed I experienced a positive feeling of revulsion. I had expected utter oblivion, the reason for shooting myself in the heart. And here I was in the grasp of a creature, of course non-human, but which *was*, which existed: 'So then there is a life beyond the grave!' I thought, with that strange levity of dreams, but the essential nature of my mind remained with me in all its intensity: 'And if I *have* to be again', thought I, 'and live again at someone's inexorable behest, then I do not want to be overmastered and humiliated!' 'You know that I am afraid of you, and that you despise me for it', I said suddenly to my companion, unable to hold back the demeaning question, which concealed an admission, and sensing my own humiliation, like the prick of a needle, in my heart. He did not reply to my question, but I had a sudden feeling that I was no longer despised or mocked, or even pitied, and that our journey had an end in view, one that was unknown and mysterious and concerned me alone. Fear grew within me. Something mutely agonized was conveyed to me by my silent companion and seemed to pierce my being. We were passing through dark, unfamiliar regions of space. I had long ceased to make out the constellations I could identify. I knew that there existed stars in the deeps of space, whose light took thousands, even millions of years to reach the earth. Perhaps we had already winged our way beyond these expanses. I was waiting for something in the anguish tormenting my heart. Then, quite suddenly, a familiar and utterly beguiling emotion shook me: I saw our sun! I knew it couldn't be *our* sun, which had given birth to *our* earth, and that we were an infinite distance from our sun, but I realized with all my being that it was exactly the same kind of sun as ours, its duplicate and double. A sweet, seductive emotion struck chords of ecstasy within my soul: my heart responded to the dear familiar power of the light which had begot me, and revived. I felt a sense of life, my former life, for the first time since my interment.

'But if this is the sun, if this is exactly the same sun as ours', I cried, 'then where is the earth?' And my companion pointed out a little star glittering like an emerald in the darkness. We were floating straight towards it.

'Surely there can't be duplications like that in the universe, can it really be a law of nature? . . . And if that is an earth over there, can it possibly be an earth just like ours? . . . Exactly the same, wretched, poor, ever-beloved—inspiring in its most ungrateful children the same poignant affection? . . .' I cried, racked with irresistible, rapturous love for that dear old former earth I had left behind. The image of the poor little girl I had wronged flashed before me.

'You will see it all', responded my companion, and a kind of grief echoed in his words.

But by now we were swiftly approaching the planet. It grew before my eyes, I could already make out the ocean and the outline of Europe, and all at once, a strange emotion as of a

great, holy jealousy flared up in my heart: 'How could there
be such a duplicate and why? I love and can only love that
earth which I have left behind, which bears the splashes of
my blood, when I, ungrateful, put out my life with a shot
through the heart. But I never, ever ceased to love that earth,
and it may be that I loved it more poignantly than ever before
on the very night I parted from it. Is there torment on this
earth? On our earth we can only truly love suffering, or
through it! We know no other way to love and know no other
kind of love. I seek to suffer in order to love. I want, I long at
this moment to kiss, bathed in tears, only that earth I have
left behind, I do not want and will not accept any other sort
of life! . . .'

But my companion had already left me. All at once I was
standing, almost without being aware of it, on that other earth
in the bright sunlight of a paradisal day. I was apparently
standing on one of the islands which on our earth make up
the Greek archipelago, or somewhere on the coast of the
mainland adjoining that archipelago. Ah, it was all exactly as
with us, but it seemed that everywhere glowed with a kind of
festive air, some great sacred triumph finally achieved. The
tender emerald sea lapped quietly against the shores, caressing them with a love which was obvious, palpable, almost
conscious. Tall, beautiful trees stood clad in the full luxuri-
ance of their blossom; their numberless leaves, I am convinced, greeted me with a low, caressing murmur, seeming to
utter words of love. The grass sparkled with bright, sweet-
smelling flowers. Flocks of birds flew across the skies, and,
quite unafraid of me, perched on my shoulders and hands
and gladly fluttered their dear little wings at me. And finally,
I saw and recognized the people of this happy earth. They
came to me of their own volition, surrounding me, kissing
me. The children of the sun, children of their own sun—ah,
how beautiful they were! Never on our earth had I seen such
beauty in a person. Perhaps only in our children, in their very
earliest years, might one have found some distant, feeble
reflection of that beauty. The eyes of these happy people
sparkled, limpid and lustrous. Their faces radiated intelligence and a kind of consciousness which had attained to the

condition of serenity, but these faces were blithe and a childlike gaiety echoed in their words and voices. Ah, at the first sight of their faces, I immediately comprehended everything, everything! It was an earth as yet undefiled by the Fall. It was inhabited by sinless people, who lived in that paradise in which, according to the tradition of all mankind, our sinful ancestors had lived—with this difference, that the entire earth here was one and the same paradise. These people, smiling gladly, crowded around me, showering me with affection; they took me to their homes and each of them sought to set me at ease. Oh, they did not ask me any questions; it was as if they knew all about it already, and they sought to drive the suffering from my face as quickly as they were able.

IV

AGAIN, you see—well, all right, so it was just a dream! But the feeling of love from those innocent, beautiful people has remained within me ever since, and I sense their love pouring down on me from yonder even now. I saw them myself, got to know them thoroughly, and was won over; I loved them and later suffered on their account. Oh, of course I realized at once, even at the time, that there was much about them that I would never comprehend fully; it seemed baffling to me, a modern progressive and vile Petersburger, that they did not possess our science, despite knowing so much. But I soon grasped that their knowledge was augmented and nourished by quite other insights than our earthly ones, and their aspirations too were altogether different. They desired nothing and were serene, they did not strive for a knowledge of life, as we do, because for them life was complete in itself. But their knowledge was both higher and more profound than our science; for our science seeks to explain what life is, seeking to comprehend it in order to teach others to live; they knew very well how to live without science and that I understood, but I could not comprehend their knowledge.

They pointed out their trees to me and I could not understand the degree of love with which they looked on them: it was as if they talked of creatures like themselves. And you know, perhaps I won't be far wrong if I say they used to talk to them! Yes, they had discovered their language and I am convinced that the trees understood them. They looked on all nature in this fashion; the animals, who lived peaceably alongside them, never attacked them—indeed loved them, tamed by the love they themselves received. They pointed out the stars to me and spoke of something beyond my comprehension, but I am certain that they were in contact with the celestial stars, not just in the intellectual sense but in some actual, physical fashion. Ah no, these people never tried to get me to understand them, they loved me without that, but I also knew that they would never comprehend me and therefore rarely spoke to them of this earth of ours. All I did was kiss the earth they lived on, and adored them wordlessly, and they saw this and allowed themselves to be adored, unembarrassed at my worship because they themselves loved so much. They were not distressed on my account when I sometimes used to kiss their feet, knowing with gladness in their hearts of the power of their reciprocal love. At times I would ask myself in astonishment: how did they contrive over all that time not to offend someone like me, and not arouse feelings of jealousy and envy in such an individual as myself? Time and again I asked myself how I, a braggart and liar, could refrain from talking to them of my own learning of which naturally they had no conception, or experience no desire to astonish them in some such fashion, if only out of the love I bore them?

They were as gay and frolicsome as children. They would roam about their beautiful woods and fields as they sang their delightful songs; they ate sparingly of the fruits of their trees, the honey of their forests, and the milk of their affectionate animals. Their food and clothing cost them only brief labour. Love was known among them and children were born, but I never came across any of those outbursts of *cruel* sensuality which affect virtually everybody on our earth, each and every one of us, and which represent the unique source of almost all the sins of mankind. They rejoiced at the children who appeared, as at new participants in their bliss. There were no quarrels between them and no jealousy; they did not even understand what that was. Their children were the children of all, because they all made up one family. They had virtually no ailments, though death did exist; the old people died peacefully, falling asleep as it were, surrounded by people bidding them farewell; they blessed them, smiling and receiving bright smiles in return. I saw no grief or tears during all this, nothing but love mounting to a pitch of ecstasy—a serene, fulfilled, contemplative ecstasy. One might even have thought that they maintained contact with those who had already passed on and that their earthly communion was not disrupted by death.

They could barely understand me when I used to ask them about eternal life, but were evidently so instinctively assured of it that it did not constitute a problem for them. They had no shrines but they did have a kind of constant, vital, living communion with the universal Whole; they had no religious creed, instead they were secure in the knowledge that when their earthly joy reached the utmost limit of earthly nature, there would come for both the living and the dead a still ampler breadth of contact with the universal Whole. They awaited that moment with gladness, but unhurriedly, without worrying themselves about it; it was as if they kept it among the emotional anticipations which they communicated to one another. Of an evening, before retiring, they enjoyed composing tuneful and harmonious choruses. In their songs, they conveyed all the emotions with which the day past had furnished them, glorifying and bidding it farewell. They hymned nature, the earth, the sea, the forests; they were fond of composing songs about each other, and praised one another like children; these songs were of the plainest but they welled out from the heart and pierced the hearts of others. Nor was it just in the songs; they seemed to pass their whole lives in feasting their eyes on one another. It was a kind of mutual love affair, complete and universal. Their other songs, solemn and rapturous, I could barely grasp. Though I understood the words, I could never penetrate the core of their meaning. It remained inaccessible to my mind, even though my heart unconsciously became increasingly suffused with it. I frequently used to tell them that I had felt a premonition of all this long ago, when back on our earth all this gladness and praise had taken the form of a seductive longing, rising at times to a pitch of unbearable grief; that I had foreseen them all and their praise in the dreams of my heart and the visions of my mind, that often I could not watch a sunset without tears ... That in my hatred towards the people of our earth there was always an element of anguish: why could I not hate them without loving them? Why couldn't I deny them forgiveness, why was there this anguish in my love: why couldn't I love them without hating them? They listened to me and I saw that they were unable to conceive what I was talking about, but I did not regret telling them about it: I knew that they understood the intensity of my anguish over those I had left behind. Yes, when they looked at me with their sweet, love-laden glances, when I felt that, among them, my heart too was becoming as innocent and truthful as theirs, I had no regrets over not understanding them. My breath failed me at the awareness of the plenitude of life, and I silently worshipped them.

Oh yes, nowadays everyone laughs in my face and assures me that in dreams one simply cannot see the sort of detail I now recount, that everything I saw or experienced in my dream was the emotions engendered by my heart in its wild imaginings, and that I added the details after I had woken up. And when I declared to them that perhaps all this had actually taken place—Lord, what laughter went up, what merriment I afforded them! Oh yes, of course I had been overwhelmed by the mere experience of that dream and that alone has survived intact in my lacerated heart: as against this, the actual images and forms of my dream, that is, those I actually saw during the time of my dream, attained such harmony, were so entracingly beautiful and so true, that when I awoke I was unable to embody them in our feeble words, so they must have become blurred in my mind, as it were, and as a consequence perhaps I myself was unconsciously forced to invent the details, naturally distorting them, especially in view of my heart's passionate desire to convey them quickly and in whatever form. On the other hand, how on earth could I not believe that it had all taken place? Prehaps it had been a thousand times better, more radiant and joyous than the way I have recounted it? It may have been a dream, but it cannot be that it did not take place. You know, I'm going to tell you a secret; all this, perhaps, was no dream at all! Because something happened, something so horribly real that it could not have been a figment in a dream. Granted, my heart gave rise to the dream, but surely my heart alone could not have engendered a reality so grim as that which I experienced? How could I alone have invented that, or my heart dreamed it into being? Surely my shallow heart and the paltry vagaries of my mind could not exalt themselves to such a revelation of truth! Oh, judge for yourselves: I have been dissembling the full truth, but I will now recount that truth also. The fact is that I . . . corrupted them all!

V

YES, yes, it ended with me corrupting them all! How this could have come about—I don't know, but my recollection is clear. My dream lasted for millennia but left in me only a general sense of the whole. All I know is that I was the cause of the Fall. Like a foul trichina, like a pestilential germ bringing contagion to whole countries, I infected that earth, happy and sinless before my arrival. They learned how to lie, and grew to love lying and perceive its beauty. Oh, it may have started off *innocently*, as a joke, in a coy way, as part of an amorous intrigue, perhaps a mere germ, but that germ of a lie penetrated their hearts and found a welcome. After that, lechery swiftly came into being, lechery begat jealousy, jealousy cruelty . . . Oh, I don't know, don't remember, but soon, very soon, the first blood was spilt: they were amazed and horror-stricken; they began to move apart and divide among themselves. Alliances formed, pitted one against another. Reproach and blame began. They learned what shame was, and shame was elevated into a virtue. The concept of honour came into being and each alliance raised its own banner. They began tormenting the animals, which fled from them into the forests and became their foes. The struggle began for separateness, isolation, personal identity, what's yours and what's mine. They began speaking different languages. They learned grief and grew to love it, they craved for suffering and said that Truth could only be attained through it. Then science appeared among them. When they became wicked, they started talking of brotherhood and humane values and grasped these concepts. When they took up criminality, they invented justice and enacted whole codes of law to preserve it, while for the maintenance of the codes they set up the guillotine.

They retained only the faintest recollection of what they had lost and had no desire to believe that they had once been innocent and happy. They derided the mere possibility of this former felicity of theirs and termed it a day-dream. They could not even picture it to themselves in images and forms, but strange and wondrous to relate, having lost any credence in their former happiness, calling it a fairy tale, they so longed to be innocent and happy once more, all over again that, childlike, they fell down before this, their heart's desire, deified it, built temples, and began to worship their own idea, their own 'desire', and tearfully bowed before it in adoration, while at the same time utterly discounting its feasibility or the possibility of its realization. However, had it ever become possible for them to return to the state of happy innocence they had lost, and if someone could have shown it to them again and asked if they wanted to return to it, they would certainly have refused. They answered me: 'What if we are mendacious, wicked, and unjust, we *know* this and deplore it, and torment ourselves on that account, we punish and torture ourselves, perhaps even more than that merciful Judge who will judge us and whose name we know not. But we have our science, and through it we will once more seek out truth, but embrace it consciously this time. Knowledge is superior to emotion, cognition of life superior to life. Science will give us wisdom, wisdom will reveal the laws, and knowledge of the

laws of happiness is happiness—nay, superior to happiness.'
Thus they spoke to me and, after these words, each one of
them plumed himself above all others, nor could they have
done otherwise. Each one had become so jealous of his own
individuality that he tried with all his might to humiliate and
belittle it in others, making it the aim of his life. Slavery
appeared, even voluntary slavery: the weak willingly subordi-
nated themselves to the strongest on condition that the latter
assisted them in oppressing those still weaker. Prophets
appeared, who went to these people in tears and told them of
their pride, their loss of proportion and harmony, their
abandonment of shame. They were laughed to scorn and
stoned.* Sacred blood was shed on temple thresholds. As
against this, people appeared who began devising ways of
bringing men together again, so that each individual, without
ceasing to prize himself above all others, might not thwart
any other, so that all might live together in harmony. Wars
were waged for the sake of this notion. All the belligerents
firmly believed at the same time that science, wisdom, and
the instinct of self-preservation would eventually compel men
to unite in a rational and harmonious society, and therefore,
to speed up the process in the mean time, 'the wise' strove
with all expedition to destroy 'the unwise' and those who
failed to grasp their idea, so that they might not hinder its
triumph.
  But the instinct of self-preservation swiftly began to
weaken; arrogant men appeared, and sensualists who baldly
demanded all or nothing. To obtain the all, they resorted to
villainy and when that did not avail—to suicide. Religions
sprang up, which preached the cult of non-existence and
self-destruction for the sake of eternal rest in nothingness. At
length, these people wearied of their senseless toil; marks of
suffering appeared on their faces, and these people pro-
claimed that suffering was beauty, because thought existed
only in suffering. They hymned suffering in their songs. I
walked among them, wringing my hands, and wept over them,
though loving them, perhaps, even more than before, when
their faces had not yet developed marks of suffering, when
they were innocent and so beautiful. I grew to love the earth

they had defiled even more than when it had been a paradise, for the sole reason that grief had appeared upon it. Alas, I had always loved sorrow and grief, but only for myself, for myself; for them I wept in my pity. I stretched out my arms to them in my despair, accusing, cursing, and despising myself. I told them that I had done all this, I alone, that I had brought them corruption, contagion, and lies! I begged them to crucify me on a cross and taught them how to make one. I could not kill myself, my strength failed me, but I wanted to be tortured by them, I craved torment, craved for my blood to be shed to the last drop during my agony. But they only laughed at me and at length began to regard me as a holy simpleton. They sought to make excuses for me, they said they had received only what they had themselves desired, and that the present situation had been inevitable. Finally, they declared that I was becoming a danger to them and they would confine me in an asylum if I did not hold my peace. At this, grief entered into my soul with such force that my heart shrank and I thought I should die, and then . . . well, that was when I woke up.

*   *   *

It was morning by now, I mean it was still not light, but it was after five. I came to in the same armchair, my candle had burned out, the captain's company was asleep, and there reigned a silence rare in our house. First of all, I bounded to my feet in the utmost astonishment; nothing of this sort had ever happened to me before, even including the trifling details: I had never dropped off to sleep in my armchair for instance. Then suddenly, as I was standing and recovering myself, suddenly I caught sight of my revolver, ready and loaded—but in a flash I pushed it away from me! Ah, now it was life, life! I raised my arms and invoked eternal truth; I did not appeal, I wept. Rapture, boundless rapture exalted my whole being. Yes, life—and preaching! That very moment, I resolved upon preaching, naturally for the whole of my life! I shall go out and preach, I want to preach—what? The truth, because I have seen it, seen it with my own eyes, seen it in all its glory!

And so, from that time forward, I have been preaching. Moreover I love those who mock me more than all the others. Why that is, I don't know and cannot explain, but so be it. They say that I am incoherent even now, meaning that if it is so now, how will it be later on? It is no more than the truth: I do get incoherent and perhaps things will get worse. And of course, I will lose track more than once before I discover how to preach—that is, what words or actions to employ, because it is a very difficult thing to do. I mean I can see all that now as clear as day: who on earth doesn't get confused? And yet everyone has the same end in view, by that I mean they are all striving towards one and the same thing, from the sage down to the last robber; they just travel by different routes. It's an old truism, but here's something new: I cannot go far wrong. Because I have seen the truth, I've seen it and know that people can be beautiful and happy, without losing their ability to live on earth. I won't accept, and refuse to believe that evil is the normal condition of men. Yet all they do is laugh at this belief of mine. But how can I not believe: I have seen the truth, my mind didn't invent it, I saw it, saw it, and its *living image* has filled my soul for ever. I have seen it in such complete wholeness that I am unable to believe it cannot exist among men. So then, how can I go astray? I will deviate of course, more than once even, and will perhaps speak in the words of others, but not for long: the living image of what I have seen will always be with me and will always correct and guide me. Oh, I am fresh and alert, and I am on my way, for a thousand years if need be. You know, at first I wanted to conceal the fact that I corrupted them all, but that was a mistake—there's my first mistake for you! But truth whispered to me that I was lying, preserved me, and set me right. But how to construct paradise—I don't know, because I can't convey it in words. After the dream, I have lost the words, at least all the chief words, the most necessary. Well, so be it: I am on my way and will keep talking ceaselessly because, after all, I saw with my own eyes, even though I can't convey what I have seen. But that's what the scoffers cannot comprehend. They say: 'He's been dreaming, he's rambling, hallucinations.' Well, what of it? And they're so proud of themselves!

Dream? What's a dream? Isn't this life of ours a dream? I'll go further: suppose it never, ever comes true, and there is no paradise (now *that* I do understand!), well, I'll still go on preaching. And yet how simple a matter it is: in one day, *in one hour* it could all be brought about, at once! The chief thing is to love others as oneself,* that's the main thing, and that's it—absolutely nothing more is necessary: you would immediately discover how to bring it about. And yet it's just the old truth after all—an old truth a billion times repeated and preached, though it fell on stony ground, didn't it? 'The cognition of life is superior to life, the knowledge of the laws of happiness—superior to happiness!—that's what has to be fought against! And I shall. If only everyone desired it, it could all be brought about at once.

*   *   *

AND I have tracked down that little girl . . . and I will go! I will!

EXPLANATORY NOTES

WHITE NIGHTS

3 *Or was he fated ... of your heart*: an inexact quotation from Turgenev's poem 'The Flower'.

5 *painted the colour of the celestial empire*: the celestial empire was the ancient name of China, whose flag bore the dragon on a yellow background.

6 *The denizens of Kamenny ... imperturbable good humour*: this refers to the villa and summer cottage developments of Petersburg. Kamenny Island and the Peterhof Road were the residences of high society. Aptekarsky Island was rather less aristocratic. Krestovsky Island was relatively undeveloped, while Pargolovo was the haunt of less well off citizens.

8 *My way led along a canal*: the action of *White Nights* takes place on the embankment of the Yekaterinsky Canal (now the Griboedov Canal).

19 *that spirit of King Solomon's*: the story of the fisherman in the *Thousand and One Nights* recounts how the prophet Allah Suleiman (the Arabic version of King Solomon) imprisoned a disobedient Djinn inside a pitcher and stopped it up with lead. After placing his magic seal on it, he threw it into the sea. A fisherman chances to haul up the pitcher and open it 1,800 years later.

20 *'The Goddess of Imagination'*: a reference to Zhukovsky's poem 'My Goddess', itself a free translation of Goethe's 'Mein Göttlin'.

22 *Hoffman*: E. T. A. Hoffmann, the German romantic writer; *Saint Bartholomew's night*: a reference to the Paris massacre of Huguenots by the Catholics on 24 August 1572; *Diana Vernon*: heroine of Sir Walter Scott's novel *Rob Roy*; *Ivan the Terrible's heroic Part ...* an allusion to the capture of Kazan from the Tartars in 1552. The episode occurs in Book IX of Karamzin's *History of the Russian State*, one of Dostoevsky's favourite books; *Clara Mowbray*: the heroine of Sir Walter Scott's novel *St Ronan's Well*; *Effie Deans*: the heroine of Scott's novel *The Heart of Midlothian*; *Huss before the Council of Prelates*: John Huss (1369–1415) was the leader of the Czech reformation, burnt at the stake as a heretic; *the rising of the dead*: an allusion to

Meyerbeer's opera *Robert le Diable*; *Minna*: this may refer to Lessing's well-known play *Minna von Barnhelm*; *Brenda*: possibly alludes to a ballad by I. I. Kozlov; *the battle on the Berezina*: the celebrated struggle at the crossing of the River Berezina at the end of 1812, which saw the Napoleonic forces finally driven from Russian soil; *the home of the Countess V—— D——*: the reference here is evidently to the Countess Vorontsova-Dashkova (1743–1810), president of the Russian Academy and the Academy of Sciences, friend of Derzhavin, Fonvizin, and many other luminaries; *Danton*; the prominent French revolutionary leader; *Cleopatra ei suoi amanti*: this was the theme suggested to the improviser in Pushkin's story *Egyptian Nights*; *the little house in Kolomna*: refers to the Pushkin poem of that title.

23 *Have they not really and truly passed*: for the remainder of this paragraph, Dostoevsky interweaves allusions to Heine's 'sie liebten sich beide', in Lermontov's translation, with the Gothic gloom of E. T. A. Hoffman's *Das Majorat* and other works of that nature from the late eighteenth and early nineteenth centuries.

37 *'R,o – Ro, s,i – si, n,a – na*: a reference to the second act of Rossini's *The Barber of Seville*, where Figaro is advising Rosina to write to her beloved, as she hands him a letter to Count Almaviva which has been prepared in advance.

A GENTLE CREATURE

61 *gros de Naples*: this was a thick, silken material.

62 *'Discipline . . . discipline'*: an inexact quotation from Gogol's story 'The Overcoat'.

Mozer: the name of this pawnbroker (and that of Dobronravov) is invented. Dostoevsky had rented a room from the Mosers in Ems in 1875.

73 *'first impressions of existence'*: this is an inexact quotation from Pushkin's poem 'The Demon'.

the fire in the blood . . . energy: an inexact quotation from a poem by Lermontov.

74 *The Pursuit of Happiness*: a drama by P. I. Yurkevich; *Songbirds*: this is the Russian title of Offenbach's operetta *La Perichole*.

75 *Mill*: the work referred to is John Stuart Mill's *The Subjection of Women* (1869), translated into Russian that year.

76 *basta!*: enough! (Spanish and Italian). Here the sense is that
    nothing else mattered beyond the pawnshop.

80 *the Vyazemsky House*: this was a home for the destitute.

93 *Politseisky Bridge*: this bridge is where Nevsky Prospect crosses
    the River Moika in Petersburg. It was renamed Narodny Bridge
    in Soviet times.

97 *Gil Blas and the Archbishop of Grenada*: a reference to a scene in
    Gil Blas, the picaresque novel by Lesage (1668–1747), where
    the hero ventures to criticize a sermon by the Archbishop. This
    scene was a favourite with Dostoevsky.

103 *'People, love one another!'* an allusion to John 15: 12 and 17. The
    fact that the hero, familiar though he is with Goethe's *Faust*
    and John Stuart Mill, cannot recall who said this, hints strongly
    at his atheism. He is also unable to pray.

THE DREAM OF A RIDICULOUS MAN

110 *droshky*: a light, four-wheeled covered carriage. Properly it
    consists of two sets of wheels joined by a board. This forms a
    seat for the passengers, who sit sideways, while the driver sits
    astride in front.

111 *shtos*: or shtoss; known as stuss in anglophone countries. This
    is a simplified form of the card-game faro. Faro itself was a
    favourite with high society gamblers from the late eighteenth to
    the early nineteenth centuries, and subsequently had a great
    vogue in the United States. Nikolai Rostov loses his fortune at
    faro in Tolstoy's *War and Peace*.

112 *But then if I should kill myself* . . . : this notion and the
    subsequent hypothesis involving the moon are very similar to
    Stavrogin's musings in Dostoevsky's earlier novel, *Devils*.

113 *Dreams, as we know, are extremely strange things*: Dostoevsky's
    thoughts on dreams in this story develop ideas on the nature
    and psychology of dreams found earlier in the novels *Crime and
    Punishment* and *The Idiot*. They also contain autobiographical
    elements: Dostoevsky frequently dreamed of his dead elder
    brother, Mikhail.

125 *Prophets appeared . . . stoned*: these biblical allusions are insepar-
    ably linked for Dostoevsky with Lermontov's bitter poem 'The
    Prophet'.

128 *The chief thing is to love others as oneself*: a reference to Mark 12:
    31.